TIME FOR A
RHYME

Chosen by Fiona Waters

Illustrated by Ailie Busby

Orion
Children's Books

For Naomi Lewis, with much love and respect   F.W.
For my parents, Irene and Gerard A.B.

First published in Great Britain in 1999
by Orion Children's Books
a division of the Orion Publishing Group Ltd
Orion House, 5 Upper St Martin's Lane,
London WC2H 9EA

This collection © Fiona Waters 1999
Illustrations © Ailie Busby 1999

Designed by Tracey Cunnell

The right of Fiona Waters, each individual author and Ailie Busby
to be identified as the compiler, authors and illustrator
respectively of this work has been asserted.

Acknowledgements on page 256

A catalogue record for this book is available from the British Library

Printed in Singapore

Hello! I'm the wizard! And it's time for a rhyme!

The wonderful thing about poetry is that when you read a poem you like, it will stay in your head so you can remember it again any time – in the bath, in the car, at breakfast time or bedtime or in between. It's fun not just to read poems in a book but to say them aloud, too.

Some poems will make you laugh because they tell you something funny, some tell a story, some are magic, and the best ones make you stop and think about things in a new way. Some you may not like at all – and some of them will seem as if the person who wrote them was writing just for you.

To help you choose what to read, look at the next page. The poems are in groups, so that if you feel like it you can read several of the same kind at once. At the end of the book there is an index giving the first lines and titles of the poems and the poets' names, so it's easy to find your favourites again.

Just for fun, there are all sorts of extra things to look for in the poems and pictures. Look at the next page to see what they are. And at the end of the book there's something else to do.

See you on the last page!

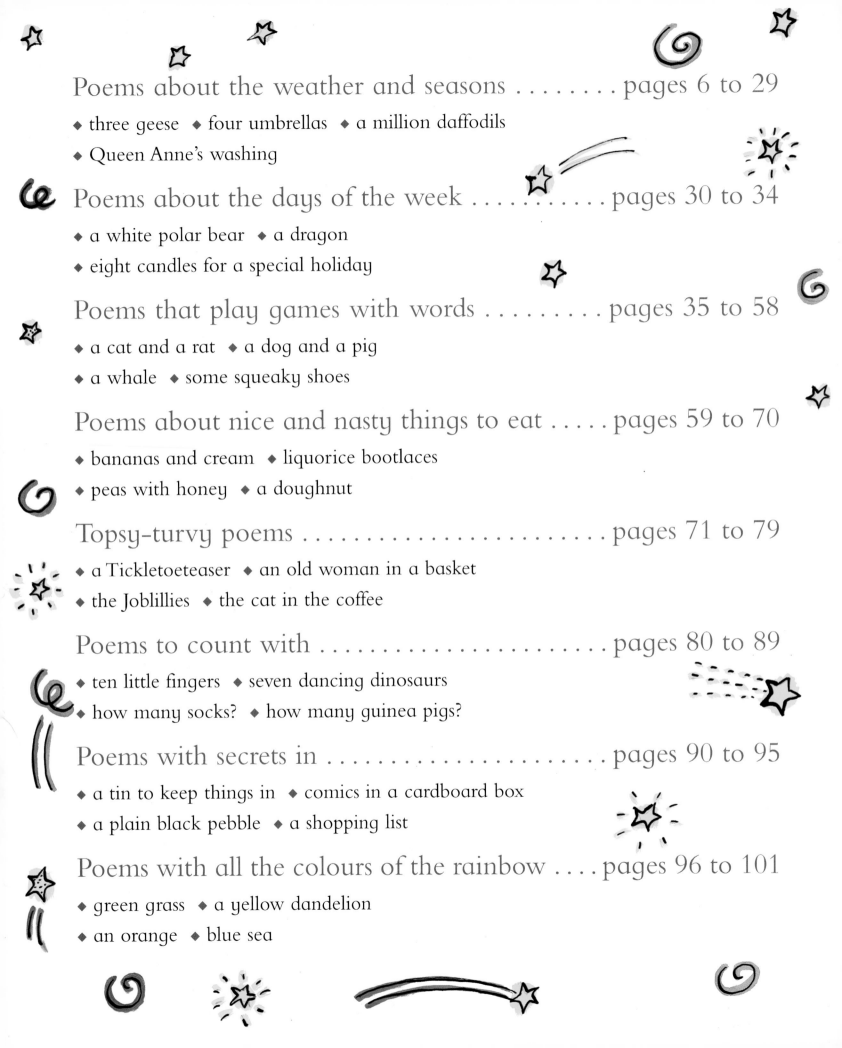

FOUR SEASONS

Spring: is showery, flowery, bowery.

Summer: hoppy, choppy, poppy.

Autumn: wheezy, sneezy, freezy.

Winter: slippy, drippy, nippy.

Anonymous

March winds and April showers
Bring forth May flowers.

Anonymous

Red sky at night,
Shepherd's delight;
Red sky in the morning,
Shepherd's warning.

Anonymous

Come the oak before the ash,
My lady's sure to wear her sash;
Come the ash before the oak,
My lady's sure to wear her cloak.

Anonymous

If bees stay at home,
The rain will soon come;
If bees fly away,
It'll be a fine day.

Anonymous

Cock Robin got up early
At the break of day,
And went to Jenny's window
To sing a roundelay.
He sang Cock Robin's love
To the little Jenny Wren,
And when he got unto the end,
Then he began again.

Anonymous

WEATHER

Whether the weather be fine,
Or whether the weather be not,
Whether the weather be cold,
Or whether the weather be hot,
We'll weather the weather
Whatever the weather,
Whether we like it or not!

Anonymous

ONE MISTY, MOISTY MORNING

One misty, moisty morning,
When cloudy was the weather,
I chanced to meet an old man,
Clothed all in leather.
He began to compliment
And I began to grin.
How do you do? And how do you do?
And how do you do again?

Anonymous

Hinty, minty, cuty, corn,
Apple seed, and apple thorn,
Wire briar, limber lock,
Three geese in a flock.
One flew east, and one flew west,
One flew over the cuckoo's nest.

Traditional

FISHING FOR RAINBOWS

The sky is grey.
We're fishing for rainbows
Today.

With nets on poles,
We're swishing the rainbow
Shoals.

Under the weed,
That's where the rainbows
Feed.

Rainbows in a jar,
Not sticklebacks.
They're rainbows.
They are.

Jeanne Willis

SPRING IS

Spring is when
       the morning sputters like
bacon
    and
        your
           sneakers
              run
                 down
                    the
                       stairs
so fast you can hardly keep up with them,
and
spring is when
        your scrambled eggs
           jump
              off
                the
                   plate
and turn into a million daffodils
trembling in the sunshine.

Bobbi Katz

CHILD'S SONG IN SPRING

The silver birch is a dainty lady,
She wears a satin gown;
The elm tree makes the old churchyard shady,
She will not live in town.
The English oak is a sturdy fellow,
He gets his green coat late;
The willow is smart in a suit of yellow,
While brown the beech trees wait.
Such a gay green gown God gives the larches –
As green as He is good!
The hazels hold up their arms for arches
When spring rides through the wood.
The chestnut's proud and the lilac's pretty,
The poplar's gentle and tall,
But the plane tree's kind to the poor dull city –
I love him best of all!

E Nesbit

SUSAN BLUE

Oh, Susan Blue,
How do you do?
Please may I go for a walk with you?
Where shall we go?
Oh, I know –
Down in the meadow where the cowslips grow!

Kate Greenaway

Round and round the garden
Went the teddy bear.
One step, two step,
Tickle you under there!

Traditional

A COMPARISON

Apple blossoms look like snow,
They're different, though.
Snow falls softly, but it brings
Noisy things:
Sleighs and bells, forts and fights,
Cosy nights.
But apple blossoms when they go,
White and slow,
Quiet all the orchard space
Till the place
Hushed with falling sweetness seems
Filled with dreams.

John Farra

THE MARCH WIND

I come to work as well as play;
I'll tell you what I do;
I whistle all the livelong day,
"Woo-oo-oo-oo! Woo-oo!"
I toss the branches up and down
And shake them to and fro,
I whirl the leaves in flocks of brown,
And send them high and low.
I strew the twigs upon the ground,
The frozen earth I sweep;
I blow the children round and round
And wake the flowers from sleep.

Anonymous

APRIL RAIN SONG

Let the rain kiss you.
Let the rain beat upon your head with silver liquid drops.
Let the rain sing you a lullaby.
The rain makes still pools on the sidewalk.
The rain makes running pools in the gutter.
The rain plays a little sleep-song on our roof at night –
And I love the rain.

Langston Hughes

QUEEN ANNE'S LACE

Queen Anne, Queen Anne, has washed her lace
(She chose a summer day)
And hung it in a grassy place
To whiten, if it may.

Queen Anne, Queen Anne, has left it there,
And slept the dewy night;
Then waked, to find the sunshine fair,
And all the meadows white.

Queen Anne, Queen Anne, is dead and gone
(She died a summer's day),
But left her lace to whiten on
Each weed-entangled way!

Mary Leslie Newton

MOON

"The moon is thousands of miles away,"
My Uncle Trevor said.
Why can't he see
It's caught in a tree
Above our onion bed?

Gareth Owen

OPEN HYDRANT

Water rushes up
and gushes, cooling summer's sizzle.
In a sudden whoosh
it rushes,
not a little drizzle.

First a hush and down
it crashes,
over curbs it swishes.

Just a luscious waterfall
for
cooling city fishes.

Marci Ridlon

15

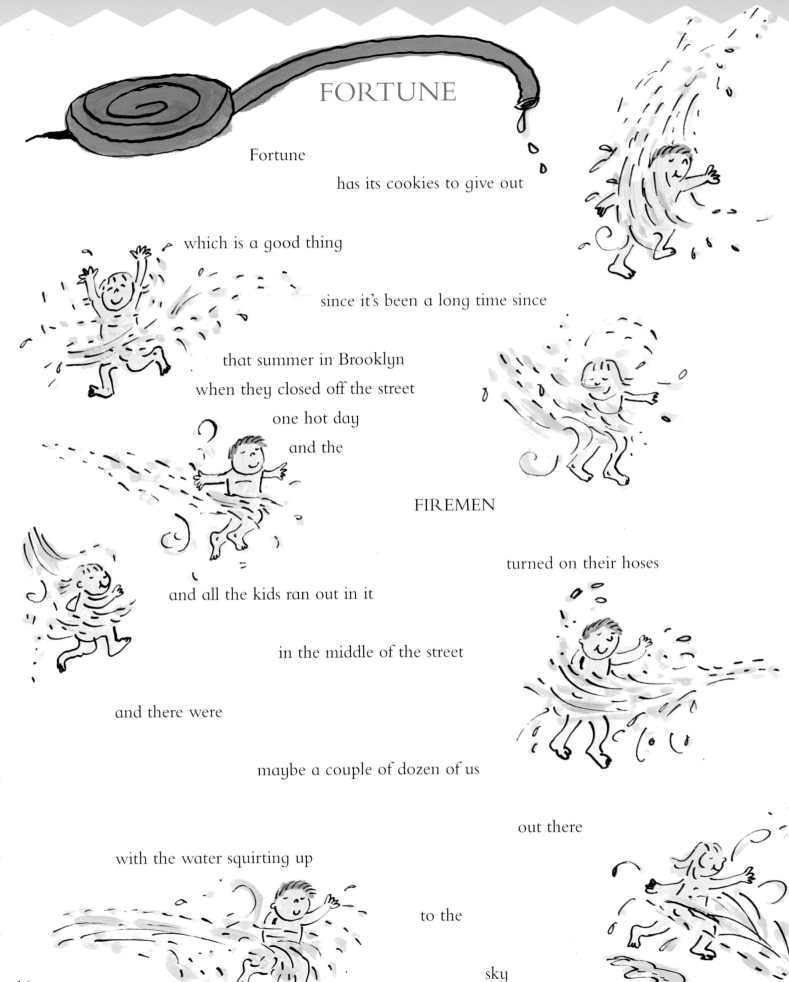

FORTUNE

Fortune

    has its cookies to give out

which is a good thing

    since it's been a long time since

    that summer in Brooklyn
when they closed off the street
    one hot day
    and the

FIREMEN

    turned on their hoses

and all the kids ran out in it

    in the middle of the street

and there were

    maybe a couple of dozen of us

    out there

with the water squirting up

    to the

    sky

and all over

us

there was maybe only six of us

kids altogether

running around in our

barefeet and birthday

suits

and I remember Molly but then

the firemen stopped squirting their hoses

all of a sudden and went

back in

their firehouse

and

started playing pinochle again

just as if nothing

had ever

happened

While I remember Molly

looked at me and

ran in

because I guess really we were the only ones there

Lawrence Ferlinghetti

DIDN'T IT RAIN

Now, didn't it rain, chillun,
God's gonna destroy this world with water,
Now didn't it rain, my Lord,
Now didn't it rain, rain, rain.

Well, it rained forty days and it rained forty nights,
There wasn't no land nowhere in sight,
God sent a raven to carry the news,
He lifted his wings and away he flew.

Well, it rained forty days and forty nights without stopping,
Noah was glad when the rain stopped a-dropping.
God sent Noah a rainbow sign,
Says, "No more water, but fire next time."

They knocked at the window and they knocked at the door,
They cried, "O Noah, please take me on board."
Noah cried, "You're full of sin,
The Lord's got the key and you can't get in."

Traditional American

THE RAIN HAS SILVER SANDALS

The rain has silver sandals
For dancing in the spring,
And shoes with golden tassels
For summer's frolicking.
Her winter boots have hobnails
Of ice from heel to toe,
Which now and then she changes
For moccasins of snow.

Mary Justus

LITTLE RAINDROPS

Oh, where do you come from,
You little drops of rain,
Pitter patter, pitter patter,
Down the window pane?

The little raindrops cannot speak,
But "pitter patter pat"
Means, "We can play on this side,
Why can't you play on *that*?"

Jane Euphemia Browne

WEATHER

Dot a dot dot dot a dot dot
Spotting the windowpane.
Spack a spack speck flick a flack fleck
Freckling the windowpane.

A spatter a scatter a wet cat a clatter
A splatter a rumble outside.
Umbrella umbrella umbrella umbrella
Bumbershoot barrel of rain.

Slosh a galosh slosh a galosh
Slither and slather a glide
A puddle a jump a puddle a jump
A puddle a pump aluddle a dump a
Puddmuddle jump in and slide!

Eve Merriam

What did the blackbird say to the crow?
"It ain't gonna rain no more."
How the heck can I wash my neck
If it ain't gonna rain no more?

Anonymous

THREE LITTLE GIRLS

Three little girls were sitting on a rail,

Sitting on a rail,

Sitting on a rail;

Three little girls were sitting on a rail,

On a fine hot day in September.

What did they talk about that fine day,

That fine day,

That fine day?

What did they talk about that fine day,

That fine hot day in September?

The crows and the corn they talked about,

Talked about,

Talked about;

But nobody knows what was said by the crows,

On that fine hot day in September.

Kate Greenaway

I hear thunder, I hear thunder;
Hark, don't you, hark, don't you?
Pitter-patter raindrops,
Pitter-patter raindrops,
I'm wet through,
I'm wet through.

I see blue skies, I see blue skies
Way up high, way up high;
Hurry up the sunshine,
Hurry up the sunshine,
We'll soon dry,
We'll soon dry!

Traditional

THE SOUND OF THE WIND

The wind has such a rainy sound
Moaning through the town,
The sea has such a windy sound –
Will the ships go down?

The apples in the orchard
Tumble from their tree –
Oh will the ships go down, go down,
In the windy sea?

Christina Rossetti

THE STORM

See lightning is flashing,
The forest is crashing,
The rain will come dashing,
A flood will be rising anon;
The heavens are scowling,
The thunder is growling,
The loud winds are howling,
The storm has come suddenly on!
But now the sky clears,
The bright sun appears,
Now nobody fears,
But soon every cloud will be gone.

Sara Coleridge

23

THIS IS HALLOWEEN

Goblins on the doorstep,
Phantoms in the air,
Owls on witches' gateposts
Giving stare for stare,
Cats on flying broomsticks,
Bats against the moon,
Stirrings round of fate-cakes
With a solemn spoon,
Whirling apple parings,
Figures draped in sheets
Dodging, disappearing,
Up and down the streets,
Jack-o'-lanterns grinning,
Shadows on a screen,
Shrieks and starts and laughter –
This is Halloween!

Dorothy Brown Thompson

NOVEMBER NIGHT

Listen . . .
With faint dry sound,
Like steps of passing ghosts,
The leaves, frost-crisped, break from the trees
And fall.

Adelaide Crapsey

WINDSHIELD WIPER

fog smog   fog smog
tissue paper   tissue paper
clear the blear   clear the smear

fog more   fog more
splat splat   downpour
rubber scraper   rubber scraper
overshoes   macintosh
bumbershoot   muddle on
slosh through   slosh through

drying up   drying up
sky lighter   sky lighter
nearly clear   nearly clear
clearing clearing veer
clear here clear

Eve Merriam

WELLIE WEATHER

Steamed-up rainy pane days
Twirling weather-vane days
Red-hot fingered chilblain days –
        Wellie weather.

Icy underfoot days
Snow transformed to soot days
All mothers' scold and tut days –
        Wellie weather.

Shivering stray cat days
"Don't forget your hat!" days
Nice children turned to brats days –
        Wellie weather.

Half the class away days
Games-field turned to clay days
Indoor dinner-time play days –
        Wellie weather.

Gas-fire turned up to three days
Scalding-hot soup for tea days
Watching far too much TV days –
        Wellie weather!

Jacqueline Brown

WINTER DAYS

Biting air
Winds blow
City streets
Under snow

Noses red
Lips sore
Runny eyes
Hands raw

Chimneys smoke
Cars crawl
Piled snow
On garden wall

Slush in gutters
Ice in lanes
Frosty patterns
On window panes

Morning call
Lift up head
Nipped by winter
Stay in bed

Gareth Owen

SNOW

No breath of wind,
No gleam of sun –
Still the white snow
Whirls softly down –
Twig and bough
And blade and thorn
All in an icy
Quiet, forlorn.
Whispering, rustling,
Through the air,
On sill and stone,
Roof – everywhere,
It heaps its powdery
Crystal flakes,
Of every tree
A mountain makes;
Till pale and faint
At shut of day
Stoops from the West
One wintry ray.
And, feathered in fire,
Where ghosts the moon,
A robin shrills
His lonely tune.

Walter de la Mare

WHITE SEASON

In the winter the rabbits match their pelts to the earth,
With ears laid back, they go
Blown through the silver hollow, the silver thicket,
Like puffs of snow.

Frances Frost

28

FREEZE

The windowsill has grown a beard

c   c
i   i
c   c
l   l
e   e

caps

Milk bottles raise their

While puddles c r a c k like broken glass

And trees wear furry w raps.

Sue Cowling

MONDAY'S CHILD IS FAIR OF FACE

Monday's child is fair of face,

Tuesday's child is full of grace,

Wednesday's child is full of woe,

Thursday's child has far to go,

Friday's child is loving and giving,

Saturday's child works hard for a living,

And the child that is born on the Sabbath day

Is bonny and blithe, and good and gay.

Anonymous

MY REAL BIRTHDAY

Birthdays come round once a year

That's not quite true of mine.

My birthday falls in Leap Year

On February twenty-nine.

Four years ago, when I was born

My life had just begun.

This is my FIRST real birthday

But I am *four* – not one.

I have a birthday every year

So I grow up on time.

But my *real* one's every four years,

On February twenty-nine.

Georgie Adams

GET UP, GET UP

Get up, get up, you lazy-head,

Get up you lazy sinner,

We need those sheets for tablecloths.

It's nearly time for dinner!

Anonymous

MY TRUE LOVE

On Monday, Monday,

My True Love said to me, "I've brought you this nice pumpkin;

I picked it off a tree!"

On Tuesday, Tuesday,

My True Love said to me, "Look – I've brought you sand tarts;

I got them by the sea."

On Wednesday, Wednesday,

My True Love said to me,

"I've caught you this white polar bear;

It came from Tennessee."

On Thursday, Thursday,

My True Love said to me,

"This singing yellow butterfly

I've all for you, from me."

On Friday, Friday,

My True Love said to me, "Here's a long-tailed guinea pig;

It's frisky as can be."

On Saturday, Saturday,

To my True Love I said,

"You have not told me ONE TRUE THING,

So you I'll never wed!"

Ivy O Eastwick

I WOKE UP THIS MORNING

I woke up this morning
at quarter past seven
I kicked up the covers
and stuck out my toe.
And ever since then
(That's a quarter past seven)
They haven't said anything
Other than "no".

They haven't said anything
Other than "Please, dear,
Don't do what you're doing,"
Or "Lower your voice."
And however I've chosen,
I've done the wrong thing
And I've made the wrong choice.

I didn't wash well
And I didn't say thank you.
I didn't shake hands
And I didn't say please.
I didn't say sorry
When, passing the candy,
I banged the box into
Miss Witelson's knees.

I didn't say sorry.
I didn't stand straighter.
I didn't speak louder
When asked what I'd said.
Well, I said
That tomorrow
At quarter past seven,
They can
Come in and get me
I'M STAYING IN BED.

Karla Kuskin

LIGHT THE FESTIVE CANDLES

(for Hanukkah)

Light the first of eight tonight –
the farthest candle to the right.

Light the first and second, too,
when tomorrow's day is through.

Then light three, and then light four –
every dusk one candle more

Till all eight burn bright and high,
honouring a day gone by

When the Temple was restored,
rescued from the Syrian lord,

And an eight-day feast proclaimed –
The Festival of Lights – well named

To celebrate the joyous day
when we regained the right to pray
to our one God in our own way.

Aileen Fisher

BREAD AND MILK FOR BREAKFAST

Bread and milk for breakfast
And woollen frocks to wear,
And a crumb for robin redbreast
On the cold days of the year.

Christina Rossetti

POSTBOX

When Poppy posted
Pappy's post
She slyly peered within
And what a shock
Poor Poppy got
When a long hand
Pulled her in!

Gareth Owen

WHAT A TO-DO

What a to-do to die today
At a minute or two to two.
A thing distinctly hard to say,
But harder still to do.
For they beat a tattoo at twenty to two
Arrattatatatatatatatatatoo
And the dragon will come
When he hears the drum
At a minute or two to two today
At a minute or two to two.

Anonymous

THIS IS THE KEY

This is the key of the kingdom
In that Kingdom is a city;
In that city is a town;
In that town there is a street;
In that street there winds a lane;
In that lane there is a yard;
In that yard there is a house;
In that house there waits a room
In that room an empty bed;
And on that bed a basket –
A basket of sweet flowers:
Of flowers, of flowers;
A basket of sweet flowers.

Flowers in a basket;
Basket on the bed;
Bed in the chamber;
Chamber in the house;
House in the weedy yard;
Yard in the winding lane;
Lane in the broad street;
Street in the high town;
Town in the city;
City in the kingdom –
This is the key of the kingdom.
Of the kingdom this is the key.

Traditional

WONDERS OF NATURE

My grandmother said, "Now isn't it queer,
That boys must whistle and girls must sing?
But that's how it is!" I heard her say –
"The same tomorrow as yesterday."

Grandmother said, when I asked her why
Girls couldn't whistle the same as I,
"Son, you know it's a natural thing –
Boys just whistle, and girls just sing."

Anonymous

MRS MASON'S BASIN

Mrs Mason bought a basin,
Mrs Tyson said, "What a nice 'un,"
"What did it cost?" said Mrs Frost,
"Half a crown," said Mrs Brown,
"Did it indeed?" said Mrs Reed,
"It did for certain," said Mrs Burton.
Then Mrs Nix up to her tricks
Threw the basin on the bricks.

Anonymous

Out goes the rat,
Out goes the cat,
Out goes the lady
With the big green hat.
Y, O, U, spells you;
O, U, T, spells out!

Traditional

HIGGLETY, PIGGLETY, POP!

Higglety, pigglety, pop!
The dog has eaten the mop;
The pig's in a hurry,
The cat's in a flurry,
Higglety, pigglety, pop!

Samuel Griswold Goodrich

MISS POLLY

Miss Polly had a dolly
Who was sick, sick, sick,
So she called for the doctor
To come quick, quick, quick.

The doctor came
With his bag and his hat,
and he knocked on the door
With a rat-tat-tat!

He looked at the dolly
And he shook his head,
He said, "Miss Polly,
Put her straight to bed."

He wrote on a paper
For a pill, pill, pill.
"I'll be back in the morning
With my bill, bill, bill."

Anonymous

THERE WAS AN OLD WOMAN

There was an old woman, who rode on a broom,
    With a high gee ho! gee humble,
And she took her tom cat behind for a groom,
    With a bimble, bamble, bumble.

They travelled along till they came to the sky,
    With a high gee ho! gee humble,
But the journey so long made them very hungry,
    With a bimble, bamble, bumble.

Says Tom, "I can find nothing here to eat,"
    With a high gee ho! gee humble,
"So let go us back again, I entreat!"
    With a bimble, bamble, bumble.

The old woman would not go back so soon,
    With a high gee ho! gee humble,
For she wanted to visit the man in the moon,
    With a bimble, bamble, bumble.

"Then," says Tom, "I'll go back by myself to our house,"
    With a high gee ho! gee humble,
"For there I can catch a good rat or a mouse,"
    With a bimble, bamble, bumble.

"But," says the old woman, "how will you go?"
    With a high gee ho! gee humble,
"You shan't have my nag, I protest and vow!"
    With a bimble, bamble, bumble.

"No, no," says Old Tom, "I've a plan of my own,"
    With a high gee ho! gee humble.
So he slid down the rainbow, and left her alone,
    With a bimble, bamble, bumble.

Anonymous

THE CENTRAL HEATING

There's a monster haunts our house –
It's called the central heating.
From the way its stomach rumbles,
Goodness knows what it's been eating!

It wakes us up at night-time
With its gurglings and its groanings,
Its clattering and its clanging,
Its mutterings and moanings.

Mum says it lives on water,
In answer to my question.
I think that it must gulp it down
To get such indigestion!

John Foster

LITTLE CHARLIE CHIPMUNK

Little Charlie Chipmunk was a talker. Mercy me!
He chattered after breakfast and he chattered after tea!
He chattered to his father and he chattered to his mother!
He chattered to his sister and he chattered to his brother!
He chattered till his family was almost driven wild.
Oh, little Charlie Chipmunk was a very tiresome child!

Helen Cowles Le Cron

There was a crooked man,
And he went a crooked mile,
He found a crooked sixpence,
Beside a crooked stile;
He bought a crooked cat,
That caught a crooked mouse,
And they all lived together
In a little crooked house.

Anonymous

THE MODERN HIAWATHA

He killed the noble Mudjokovis,
With the skin he made him mittens,
Made them with the fur side inside,
Made them with the skin side outside,
He, to get the warm side inside,
Put the inside skin side outside:
He, to get the cold side outside,
Put the warm side fur side inside:
That's why he put the fur side inside,
Why he put the skin side outside,
Why he turned them inside outside.

George A Strong

41

DANCE

I love to dance dance
juk up juk up me shoulders
twissy twassy me waist
scrinchy scrinch up me face
bouncy me feet to the beat
I love to dance dance
would you like to join me?

Pauline Stewart

BIRTH OF A SONG

It was a winter night in the
   dark season.
While others lay asleep,
A sound approached.
It hit my ear,
It hit my ear!

Inuit Traditional Song

PEOPLE

Some people talk and talk
and never say a thing.
Some people look at you
and birds begin to sing.

Some people laugh and laugh
and yet you want to cry.
Some people touch your hand
and music fills the sky.

Charlotte Zolotow

DUSTMAN

Every Thursday morning,
Before you're quite awake,
Without the slightest warning
The house begins to shake
With a Biff! Bang!
Biff! Bang! Bash!

It's the dustman, who begins
(Bang! Crash!)
To empty both the bins
Of their rubbish and their ash,
With a Biff! Bang!
Biff! Bang! Bash!

Clive Samson

RACING THE WIND

eyes staring
nostrils flaring

   feet dancing
   legs prancing

      manes flowing
      tails blowing

         hooves pacing
         horses racing

Moira Andrew

I love you, I love you,
I love you lots.
My love for you
Would fill all the pots,
Buckets, pitchers, kettles and cans,
The big washtub and both dishpans.

Anonymous

SULK

I scuff
            my feet along
And puff
            my lower lip
I sip my milk
            in slurps
And huff
And frown
And stamp around
And tip my chair
            back from the table
Nearly fall down
            But I don't care
I scuff
And puff
And frown
And huff
And stamp
And pout
Till I forget
What it's about

Felice Holman

NOISE

Billy is blowing his trumpet;
Bertie is banging a tin;
Betty is crying for Mummy
And Bob has pricked Ben with a pin.
Baby is crying out loudly;
He's out on the lawn in his pram.
I am the only one silent
And I've eaten all of the jam.

Anonymous

WHAT ARE YOU?

I am a gold lock;

I am a silver lock;

I am a brass lock;

I am a lead lock;

I am a monk lock;

I am a gold key.

I am a silver key.

I am a brass key.

I am a lead key.

I am a mon-key.

Traditional

HAVE YOU EVER SEEN?

Have you ever seen a sheet on a river bed?

Or a single hair from a hammer's head?

Has the foot of a mountain any toes?

And is there a pair of garden hose?

Does the needle ever wink its eye?

Why doesn't the wing of a building fly?

Can you tickle the ribs of a parasol?

Or open the trunk of a tree at all?

Are the teeth of a rake ever going to bite?

Have the hands of a clock any left or right?

Can the garden plot be deep and dark?

And what is the sound of the birch's bark?

Anonymous

GOOSE, MOOSE & SPRUCE

Three gooses: geese.

Three mooses: meese?

Three spruces: spreece?

Little goose: gosling.

Little moose: mosling?

Little spruce: sprosling?

David McCord

48

CHOOSING SHOES

New shoes, new shoes,
Red and pink and blue shoes.
Tell me, what would you choose,
If they'd let us buy?

Buckle shoes, bow shoes,
Pretty pointy-toe shoes,
Strappy, cappy low shoes;
Let's have some to try.

Bright shoes, white shoes,
Dandy-dance-by-night shoes,
Perhaps-a-little-tight shoes,
Like some? So would I.

But

Flat shoes, fat shoes,
Stump-along-like-that shoes,
Wipe-them-on-the-mat shoes,
That's the sort they'll buy.

Ffreda Wolfe

Oh, Mary Murple, Murple, Murple,
Dressed in purple, purple, purple,
With silver buttons, buttons, buttons
Down her girdle, girdle, girdle,
She asked her mother, mother, mother,
For fifty cents, cents, cents
To see an elephant, elephant, elephant
Jump the fence, fence, fence.
He jumped so high, high, high
He hit the sky, sky, sky
And never got back, back, back
Till the Fourth of July, ly, ly.

Anonymous

NAMES OF SCOTTISH ISLANDS TO BE SHOUTED IN A BUS QUEUE WHEN YOU'RE FEELING BORED

Yell!

Muck!

Eigg!

Rhum!

Unst!

Hoy!

Foula!

Coll!

Canna!

Barra!

Gigha!

Jura!

Pabay!

Raasay!

Skye!

Ian McMillan

WHAT SOME PEOPLE DO

Jibber, jabber, gabble, babble,
Cackle, clack and prate,
Twiddle, twaddle, mutter, stutter,
Utter, splutter, blate . . .

Chatter, patter, tattle, prattle,
Chew the rag and crack,
Spiel and spout and spit it out,
Tell the world and quack . . .

Sniffle, snuffle, drawl and bawl,
Snicker, snort and snap,
Bark and buzz and yap and yelp,
Chin and chirp and chat . . .

Shout and shoot and gargle, gasp,
Gab and gag and groan,
Hem and haw and work the jaw,
Grumble, mumble, moan . . .

Beef and bellyache and bat,
Say a mouthful, squawk,
That is what some people do
When they merely talk.

Anonymous

THE WHEELS ON THE BUS

The wheels on the bus go round and round, round and round, round and round,
The wheels on the bus go round and round, all through the town.

The people on the bus bounce up and down, up and down, up and down,
The people on the bus bounce up and down, all through the town.

The driver on the bus yells "Move on back, move on back, move on back,"
The driver on the bus yells "Move on back," all through the town.

The horn on the bus goes beep, beep, beep; beep, beep, beep; beep, beep, beep,
The horn on the bus goes beep, beep, beep, all through the town.

The wipers on the bus go swish, swish, swish; swish, swish, swish; swish, swish, swish,
The wipers on the bus go swish, swish, swish, all through the town.

The children on the bus go wiggle, wiggle, wiggle; wiggle, wiggle, wiggle; wiggle, wiggle, wiggle,
The children on the bus go wiggle, wiggle, wiggle, all through the town.

Anonymous

Eenie, meenie, minie, mo,
Catch a tiger by the toe,
If he hollers let him go,
Eenie, meenie, minie, mo.

Anonymous

IF ALL THE SEAS . . .

If all the seas were one sea,
What a great sea that would be!
If all the trees were one tree,
What a great tree that would be!
And if all the axes were one axe,
What a great axe that would be!
And if all the men were one man
What a great man that would be!
And if that great man took the great axe
And cut down that great tree,
And let it fall into the great sea,
What a splish-splash that would be!

Anonymous

FUNNY TALK

"Bubble," said the kettle,
"Bubble," said the pot.
"Bubble, bubble, bubble,
We are getting very hot!"

"Shall I take you off the fire?"
"No, you need not trouble.
This is just the way we talk –
Bubble, bubble, bubble!"

Anonymous

My shoes are new and squeaky shoes,
They're very shiny, creaky shoes,
I wish I had my leaky shoes
That Mummy threw away.

I liked my old brown leaky shoes
Much better than these creaky shoes,
These shiny, creaky, squeaky shoes
I've got to wear today.

Anonymous

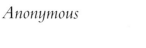

THUMPING, STUMPING, BUMPING, JUMPING

Thumping, stumping, bumping, jumping,
Ripping, nipping, tripping, skipping,
All the way home.

Popping, clopping, stopping, hopping,
Stalking, chalking, talking, walking,
All the way home.

Anonymous

55

AS WET AS A FISH

As wet as a fish – as dry as a bone;
As live as a bird – as dead as a stone;
As plump as a partridge – as poor as a rat;
As strong as a horse – as weak as a cat;
As hard as a flint – as soft as a mole;
As white as a lily – as black as a coal;
As plain as a pikestaff – as rough as a bear;
As tight as a drum – as free as the air;
As heavy as lead – as light as a feather;
As steady as time – uncertain as weather;
As hot as a furnace – as cold as a frog;
As gay as a lark – as sick as a dog;
As slow as a tortoise – as swift as the wind;
As true as the gospel – as false as mankind;
As thin as a herring – as fat as a pig;
As proud as a peacock – as blithe as a grig;

As fierce as a tiger – as mild as a dove;
As stiff as a poker – as limp as a glove;
As blind as a bat – as deaf as a post;
As cool as a cucumber – as warm as a toast;
As flat as a flounder – as round as a ball;
As blunt as a hammer – as sharp as an awl;
As red as a ferret – as safe as the stocks;
As bold as a thief – as sly as a fox;
As straight as an arrow – as bent as a bow;
As yellow as saffron – as black as a sloe;
As brittle as glass – as tough as gristle;
As neat as my nail – as clean as a whistle;
As good as a feast – as bad as a witch;
As light as is day – as dark as is pitch;
As brisk as a bee – as dull as an ass;
As full as a tick – as solid as brass.

Anonymous

IF YOU EVER

If you ever ever ever ever ever
    If you ever ever ever meet a whale
You must never never never never never
    You must never never never touch its tail:

For if you ever ever ever ever ever
    If you ever ever ever touch its tail.
You will never never never never never
    You will never never meet another whale.

Anonymous

WHISKY FRISKY

Whisky frisky.
Hipperty hop,
Up he goes
To the tree top!

Whirly, twirly,
Round and round,
Down he scampers
To the ground.

Furly, curly,
What a tail,
Tall as a feather,
Broad as a sail.

Where's his supper?
In the shell.
Snappy, cracky,
Out it fell.

Anonymous

WAITING

In the dentist's waiting room I'm

nervid

wunxious

fothered

anxit

weeful

wobbered

tummled

glumpit

frettled

horrish

gumshot

dismy

squawbid

grimlip

dregless –

IT'S ME!

Sue Cowling

DO YOU CARROT ALL FOR ME?

Do you carrot all for me?

My heart beets for you,

With your turnip nose

And your radish face,

You are a peach.

If we cantaloupe,

Lettuce marry;

Weed make a swell pear.

Anonymous

SUGARCAKE BUBBLE

Sugarcake, sugarcake
    Bubbling in a pot
Bubble, bubble sugarcake
    Bubble thick and hot

Sugarcake, sugarcake
    Spice and coconut
Sweet and sticky
    Brown and gooey

I could eat the lot.

Grace Nichols

BUT WHAT'S IN THE LARDER?

What's in the larder?
Shelves and hooks, shelves and hooks.

No bread?
Half a breakfast for a rat.

Milk?
Three laps for a cat.

Eggs?
One, but that's addled.

Alfred, Lord Tennyson

59

ROBIN THE BOBBIN

Robin the Bobbin, the big-bellied Ben,

He ate more meat than fourscore men;

He ate a crow, he ate a calf,

He ate a butcher and a half;

He ate a church, he ate a steeple,

He ate the priest and all the people!

    A cow and a calf,

    An ox and a half,

    A church and a steeple,

    And all the good people,

And yet he complained that his stomach wasn't full.

Traditional

THE DINERS IN THE KITCHEN

Our dog Fred
Et the bread

Our dog Dash
Et the hash

Our dog Pete
Et the meat

Our dog Davy
Et the gravy

Our dog Toffy
Et the coffee

And – the worst
From the first –

Our dog Fido
Et the pie-dough.

James Whitcomb Riley

60

DISASTER

I climbed up the apple tree
And all the apples fell on me;
Make a pudding, make a pie
Did you ever tell a lie?
Yes you did. You know you did.
You broke your mother's teapot lid.
She blew you in, she blew you out
You landed in the sauerkraut.

Anonymous

Humpty Dumpty sat on a wall.
He fell, so now I can see
Why all the king's horses
And all the king's men
Had scrambled egg for tea.

Finola Akister

LIQUORICE BOOTLACES

I tie my boots with liquorice.
It is a pleasant thing
To eat the pieces when they snap.
They're tastier than string.

Irene Rawnsley

A LESSON

Darren took all
the labels off
the tins in Mummy's
shopping bag.

He sorted them
like teacher had,
red and yellow,
green and blue.

Tonight the dog
had soup for tea,
the cat had beans
and Darren had

Whiskas.
He said it
tasted horrible
on toast.

Brian Morse

LOLLIPOP POEM

This poem's round
and it's stuck
on a stick.

This poem's stripey
and nice to lick.

This poem's shiny
and sticky
and sweet.

It's a lollipop poem
for anyone
to eat.

Tony Mitton

I was my mother's darling child
Brought up with care and trouble.
For fear a spoon would hurt my mouth,
She fed me with a shovel.

Anonymous

Mary had a little lamb,

A little pork, a little ham,

A little egg, a little toast,

Some pickles and a great big roast,

A lobster and some prunes,

A glass of milk, some macaroons.

It made the waiters grin

To see her order so,

And when they carried Mary out

Her face was white as snow.

Anonymous

Hot cross buns!

Hot cross buns!

One a penny, two a penny,

Hot cross buns!

If you have no daughters

Give them to your sons,

But if you haven't any of those pretty little elves

You cannot do better than eat them yourselves!

Traditional

63

BANANAS AND CREAM

Bananas and cream,
Bananas and cream:
All we could say was
Bananas and cream.

We couldn't say fruit,
We wouldn't say cow,
We didn't say sugar –
We don't say it now.

Bananas and cream,
Bananas and cream,
All we could shout was
Bananas and cream.

We didn't say why,
We didn't say how;
We forgot it was fruit,
We forgot the old cow;
We never said sugar
We only said WOW!

Bananas and cream,
Bananas and cream;
All that we want is
Bananas and cream!

We didn't say dish,
We didn't say spoon;
We said not tomorrow,
But NOW and HOW SOON

Bananas and cream,
Bananas and cream?
We yelled for bananas,
Bananas and scream!

David McCord

This little pig went to market,

This little pig stayed at home,

This little pig had roast beef,

This little pig had none,

And this little pig cried,

"Wee-wee-wee-wee-wee-wee,"

All the way home!

Traditional

PEAS

I always eat peas with honey,

I've done it all my life.

They do taste kind of funny,

But it keeps them on the knife.

Anonymous

I HAD A NICKEL

I had a nickel and I walked around the block.

I walked right into a baker shop.

I took two doughnuts right out of the grease;

I handed the lady my five-cent piece.

She looked at the nickel and she looked at me,

And said, "This money's no good to me.

There's a hole in the nickel, and it goes right through."

Says I, "There's a hole in the doughnut."

Anonymous

FIGGIE HOBBIN

Nightingales' tongues, your majesty?

Quails in aspic, cost a purse of money?

Oysters from the deep, raving sea?

Grapes and Greek honey?

Beads of black caviare from the Caspian?

Rock melon with corn on the cob in?

Take it all away! grumbled the old King of Cornwall.

Bring me some figgie hobbin!

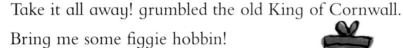

Devilled lobster, your majesty?

Scots kail brose or broth?

Grilled mackerel with gooseberry sauce?

Cider ice that melts in your mouth?

Pears filled with nut and date salad?

Christmas pudding with a tanner or a bob in?

Take it all away! groused the old King of Cornwall.

Bring me some figgie hobbin!

Amber jelly, your majesty?

Passion fruit flummery?

Pineapple sherbet, milk punch or Pavlova cake,

Sugary, summery?

Carpet-bag steak, blueberry grunt, cinnamon crescents?

Spaghetti as fine as the thread on a bobbin?

Take it all away! grizzled the old King of Cornwall.

Bring me some figgie hobbin!

So in from the kitchen came figgie hobbin,
Shining and speckled with raisins sweet,
And though on the King of Cornwall's land
The rain it fell and the wind it beat,
As soon as a forkful of figgie hobbin
Up to his lips he drew,
Over the palace a pure sun shone
And the sky was blue.
THAT'S what I wanted! He smiled, his face
Now as bright as the breast of the robin.
To cure the sickness of the heart, ah –
Bring me some figgie hobbin!

Charles Causley

POSERS

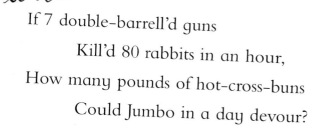

Supposing you had 6 baboons,
    And made them dance a dozen jigs,
How many pairs of pantaloons
    Would equal 50 sucking-pigs?

If every house had 7 roofs,
    And every roof 1,000 tiles,
How much is worn off horses' hoofs
    In trotting 20,000 miles?

If 60 stockings made a pair,
    And all our hats were worn in twos,
How many braces should we wear,
    Including slippers, boots and shoes?

If 20 kittens made a pie
    Of half a 100 mouses' tails,
How far is Rome from Peckham Rye
    Before the equinoctial gales?

If 40 snails could crawl a mile
    In half the time it takes to wink,
How many pills would cure the bile? –
    Please work it out in pen and ink.

If 7 double-barrell'd guns
    Kill'd 80 rabbits in an hour,
How many pounds of hot-cross-buns
    Could Jumbo in a day devour?

If every dog had 50 barks,
    And every bark 11 bites,
How many children's Noah's Arks
    Would equal 2 electric lights?

If 30 chimney-pots of ale,
    And half a looking-glass of wine,
Were all reduced to smallest scale,
    What is it multiplied by 9?

If 7 senses are confused
    By whales 600 acres long,
Why shouldn't people be amused
    At this my idiotic song?

X Parke

One, one
    Cinnamon bun

Two, two
    Chicken stew

Three, three
    Cakes and tea

Four, four
    I want more

Five, five
    Honey in a hive

Six, six
    Pretzel sticks

Seven, seven
    Straight from heaven

Eight, eight
    Clean your plate

Nine, nine
    Look at mine

Ten, ten
    Start over again!

Anonymous

OLIVER TWIST

Oliver-Oliver-Oliver Twist
Bet you a penny you can't do this:
Number one – touch your tongue
Number two – touch your shoe
Number three – touch your knee
Number four – touch the floor
Number five – stay alive
Number six – wiggle your hips
Number seven – jump to heaven
Number eight – bang the gate
Number nine – walk the line
Number ten – start again.

Traditional

The elephants are coming one by one,

Some from the moon, some from the sun,

Now they are coming two by two,

Some for me, some for you.

Here they come three by three,

Some for you, some for me,

The elephants are coming four by four,

Some through the windows, some through the floor,

Now they are coming five by five,

Some are ghosts, some are alive,

Here they come six by six,

Some on crutches, some on sticks,

The elephants are coming seven by seven,

Some from the moon, some from heaven,

Now they are coming eight by eight,

Some through the windows, some through the gate,

Here they come nine by nine,

Some are yours, some are mine …

Anonymous

GUINEA PIGS

We had two little guinea pigs
They did what guinea pigs
Have always done before
And there were four more.

    $2 \times 4 = 8 +$ the original $2 = 10$.

We had ten little guinea pigs
And they did what guinea pigs
have always done
And there were forty assorti.

    $10 \times 4 = 40 +$ the original $10 = 50$. (all colours)

We had fifty little guinea pigs
And they did what guinea pigs have always done
How can they go on and on? I wondered
And we had two hundred.

    $50 \times 4 = 200 +$ the original $50 = 250$.

Two hundred and fifty little guinea pigs
Did what they have always done
Eating us out of house and home and
There were a thousand.

    $250 \times 4 = 1000 +$ the original $250 = 1,250$.

Guinea pigs in their fluff and fur are most attractive
But I wish they were not so active
In doing what they have done before –
I can't count any more!

Rumer Godden

83

FOUR LITTLE TIGERS

Four little tigers
Sitting in a tree;
One became a lady's coat –
And now there are three.

Three little tigers
'Neath a sky of blue;
One became a rich man's rug –
Now there's only two.

Two little tigers
Sitting in the sun;
One a hunter's trophy made –
Now there's only one.

One little tiger
Waiting to be had;
Oops! He got the hunter first –
Aren't you kind of glad?

Frank Jacobs

COUNTING MAGPIES

One for sorrow,
Two for mirth
Three for a wedding,
Four for a birth,
Five for silver,
Six for gold,
Seven for a secret,
Too precious to be told!

Anonymous

TEN LITTLE FINGERS

I have ten little fingers,
And they all belong to me.
I can make them do things.
Would you like to see?

I can shut them up tight,
Or open them all wide.
I can put them all together,
Or make them all hide.

I can make them jump high,
I can make them jump low.
I can fold them quietly,
And sit just so.

Anonymous

ONE OLD OX

One old ox opening oysters,
Two toads totally tired
Trying to trot to Tewkesbury,
Three tame tigers taking tea,
Four fat friars fishing for frogs,
Five fairies finding fire-flies,
Six soldiers shooting snipe,
Seven salmon sailing in Solway,
Eight elegant engineers eating excellent eggs;
Nine nimble noblemen nibbling non-pareils,
Ten tall tinkers tasting tamarinds,
Eleven electors eating early endive,
Twelve tremendous tale-bearers telling truth.

Anonymous

TEN DANCING DINOSAURS

Ten dancing dinosaurs in a chorus line
One fell and split her skirt, then there were nine.

Nine dancing dinosaurs at a village fête
One was raffled as a prize, then there were eight.

Eight dancing dinosaurs on a pier in Devon
One fell overboard, then there were seven.

Seven dancing dinosaurs performing magic tricks
One did a vanishing act, then there were six.

Six dancing dinosaurs learning how to jive
One got twisted in a knot, then there were five.

Five dancing dinosaurs gyrating on the floor
One crashed through the floorboards, then there were four.

Four dancing dinosaurs waltzing in the sea
A mermaid kidnapped one, then there were three.

Three dancing dinosaurs head-banging in a zoo
One knocked himself out, then there were two.

Two dancing dinosaurs rocking round the sun
One collapsed from sunstroke, then there was one.

One dancing dinosaur hijacked a plane,
Flew off to Alaska and was never seen again!

John Foster

HOW MANY APPLES GROW ON THE TREE?

How many apples grow on the tree?
said Jenny.
O many many more than you can see!
said Johnny.
Even more than a hundred and three?
said Jenny.
Enough, said Johnny, for you and me
and all who eat apples from the tree
said Johnny.

How many fish swim in the sea?
said Jenny.
More than apples that grow on the tree
said Johnny.
Even more than a thousand and three?
said Jenny.
Enough, said Johnny, for you and me
and all who fish in the big blue sea
said Johnny.

George Barker

Round and round ran the wee hare.
One jump! Two jumps!
Tickle you under there.
Round about there
Sat the little hare.
The dogs came and chased him
Right up there!

Anonymous

SOCKS

Socks are so alike you can put
Either of them on either foot.

No use calling them names like Left and Right
For both of the pair are exactly alike.

Socks are twins who are always together
And never go anywhere without each other,

Together dry and together wet in the rain,
Together dirty and together clean;

You can't go out in one when the other is lost
At the back of a drawer or in the wash;

Together all day on your left leg and your right,
They're still together when you take them off at night.

Stanley Cook

THE SECRETS BOX

These are the keys
That open the locks
Of the secrets box.

This is the secrets box
Where deep inside
The stories hide.

This is the girl
Who found the keys
That open the locks
Of the secrets box.

These are the stories
Of dragons and kings,
Of wizards and rings,
Of dancing and sighs,
Of sunshine and lies.

This is the girl
Who heard the stories
From inside
And laughed and cried.

John Foster

SHOP, SHOP, SHOPPING

When Mum goes shopping
There's just no stopping
With the shop, shop, shopping.
We buy;
Hats, mats
This and thats
A watering can
Gloves for Gran
Shorts, shirts
Pants and vest
Party shoes to keep for best
Material for Mum's new dress
Finger paints to make a mess
A puzzle, too
For me to do
A potted plant –
That's for Aunt,
Some bread and cakes . . .
For goodness sakes!
PLEASE!
No more shopping
We're drop, drop, dropping
All the shop, shop, shopping!

Georgie Adams

WHAT DO YOU COLLECT?

What do you collect?
Coins, dolls from other lands?
Or jokes that no one understands?

What do you collect?
Skulls, posters, badges, bells?
Or walking sticks, or seaside shells?

What do you collect?
Stamps, gem stones, model cars?
Or wrappers torn from chocolate bars?

What do you collect?
Leaves, photographs of cats?
Or horror masks and rubber bats?

What do you collect?
Books, fossils, records, rocks?
Or comics in a cardboard box?

Wes Magee

92

TREASURE TROVE

I have a tin
to keep things in
underneath
my bedroom floor.

I put my finger
in the crack,
quietly lift
the floorboard back,

and there's my store,
safely hid
in a tin with roses
on the lid.

A few feathers
and a chicken's claw,
a big tooth
from a dinosaur,

the wrapper
from my Easter egg,
a Christmas robin
with one leg,

long hairs
from a horse's mane,
real pesetas
come from Spain,

three of my
operation stitches,
like spiders
wrapped in bandages,

a marble
full of dragon smoke,
flashing with fire
in the dark,

a magic pebble
round and white,
a sparkler left
from bonfire night.

Irene Rawnsley

93

PEBBLES

Pebbles belong to no one
Until you pick them up –
Then they are yours.

But which, of all the world's
Mountains of little broken stones,
Will you choose to keep?

The smooth black, the white,
The rough grey with sparks
Shining in its cracks?

Somewhere the best pebble must
Lie hidden, meant for you
If you can find it.

Valerie Worth

THE BLACK PEBBLE

There went three children down to the shore,
    Down to the shore and back;
There was skipping Susan and bright-eyed Sam
    And little scowling Jack.

Susan found a white cockle-shell,
    The prettiest ever seen,
And Sam picked up a piece of glass
    Rounded and smooth and green.

But Jack found only a plain black pebble
    That lay by the rolling sea,
And that was all that he ever found;
    So back they went all three.

The cockle-shell they put on the table,
    The green glass on the shelf,
But the little black pebble that Jack had found,
    He kept it for himself.

James Reeves

THE POND

I stood and watched
the smooth water
and saw myself
upside down.

The wind rose,
and suddenly
I became
a million zigzags
shimmering
in the sun.

In the morning it is green
with water lilies
like little moons
floating.

In the afternoon it is
broken into blue ripples
like ribbons.

At night
it is dark and mysterious
like a bowl
of black ink.

Charlotte Zolotow

DANDELION

Little soldier with the golden helmet,
What are you guarding on my lawn?
You with your green gun
And your yellow beard,
Why do you stand so stiff?
There is only the grass to fight!

Hilda Conkling

A COLOURFUL WORLD

Sea swirling,
waves curling
BLUE.

Desert shifting,
sand drifting
YELLOW.

Seeds sowing,
grass mowing
GREEN.

Fire burning,
flames turning
ORANGE.

Wind blowing,
clouds growing
BLACK.

Cold morning,
snow storming
WHITE.

Sun setting,
sky getting
RED.

Georgie Adams

THE BIGGEST FIREWORK

The biggest firework
Ever lit,
Fizzed, banged,
Glittered, flew
In Golden–Silver–
Red–Green–Blue.
It rocketed
So far away,
It brought to night
A burst of day,
Electric bulbs
A million bright
Of shining spray.

But of its fiery magic spell
All that is left
Is the smoke smell . . .

Anonymous

Roses are red,
Cabbages are green,
You have a shape
Like a washing machine.

Traditional

Roses are red, violets are blue,
All the sweetest flowers in the forest grew.

Traditional

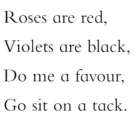

Roses are red,
Violets are black,
Do me a favour,
Go sit on a tack.

Traditional

Roses are red,
Violets are blue,
A face like yours
Belongs in the zoo.

Traditional

Roses are red, violets are blue,
Sugar is sweet and so are you.
The violets in the fall,
But you get sweeter than all.

Traditional

PAINTING

Yellow is my favourite colour;
I'm painting like the sun,
Yellow birds in golden bushes
Till all the yellow's done.

Green is my favourite colour;
I'm painting like the grass,
Green woods and fields and rushes,
The river flowing past.

Blue is my favourite colour;
I'm painting like the sea,
Blue sailing ships and fishes,
And icebergs floating free.

Red is my favourite colour;
I'm painting like a fire,
Red twigs, then blazing branches
As the flames leap higher.

Irene Rawnsley

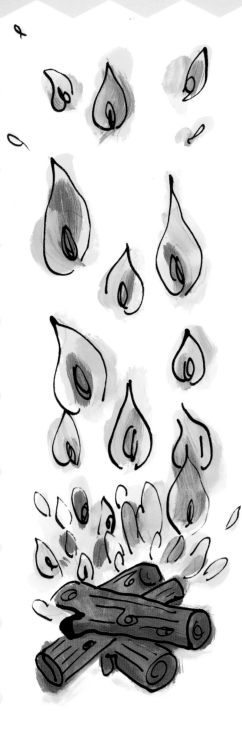

COLOURFUL MOODS

When grown-ups say, "I'm feeling BLUE,"
It really means they're sad.
Or if they say, "I'm in the PINK,"
They're healthy, bright and glad.

It's strange the things that people say
Like, envy turns you GREEN.
Or someone's turned a ghostly WHITE
At frightening things they've seen.

It's odd the colours grown-ups go
Or say that they have been.
I stay the colour of my skin
Whatever mood I'm in.

Georgie Adams

COLOURS

What is pink? A rose is pink
By the fountain's brink.
What is red? A poppy's red
In its barley bed.
What is blue? The sky is blue
Where the clouds float through.
What is white? A swan is white,
Sailing in the light.
What is yellow? Pears are yellow,
Rich and ripe and mellow.
What is green? The grass is green,
With small flowers between.
What is violet? Clouds are violet
In the summer twilight.
What is orange? Why, an orange –
Just an orange!

Christina Rossetti

TRAVEL

I should like to rise and go
Where the golden apples grow;
Where below another sky
Parrot islands anchored lie,
And, watched by cockatoos and goats,
Lonely Crusoes building boats;
Where in sunshine reaching out
Eastern cities, miles about,
Are with mosque and minaret
Among sandy gardens set,
And the rich goods from near and far
Hang for sale in the bazaar;
Where the Great Wall round China goes,
And on one side the desert blows,
And with bell and voice and rum,
Cities on the other hum;
Where are forests, hot as fire
Wide as England, tall as a spire,
Full of apes and coconuts
And the negro hunters' huts;
Where the knotty crocodile
Lies and blinks in the Nile,
And the red flamingo flies
Hunting fish before his eyes;

Where in jungles, near and far,
Man-devouring tigers are,
Lying close and giving ear
Lest the hunt be drawing near,
Or a comer-by be seen
Swinging in a palanquin;
Where among the desert sands
Some deserted city stands,
All his children, sweep and prince,
Grown to manhood ages since.
Not a foot in street or house,
Not a stir of child or mouse,
And when kindly falls the night,
In all the town no spark of light.

There I'll come when I'm a man
With a camel caravan;
Light a fire in the gloom
Of some dusty dining-room;
See the pictures on the walls,
Heroes, fights and festivals;
And in corner find the toys
Of the old Egyptian boys.

Robert Louis Stevenson

I SAW A SHIP A-SAILING

I saw a ship a-sailing,
A-sailing on the sea;
And oh! it was laden
With pretty things for me.

There were comfits in the cabin,
And apples in the hold;
The sails were made of silk,
And the masts were made of gold.

The four-and-twenty sailors
That stood between the decks,
Were four-and-twenty white mice,
With chains about their necks.

The Captain was a duck,
With a packet on his back,
And when the ship began to move,
The Captain said, "Quack, quack!"

Anonymous

THE CAVE-BOY

I dreamed I was a cave-boy
And lived in a cave,
A mammoth for my saddle horse,
A monkey for my slave.
And through the tree-fern forests
A-riding I would go,
When I was once a cave-boy,
A million years ago.

I dreamed I was a cave-boy;
I hunted with a spear
The sabre-toothed tiger,
The prehistoric deer.
A wolf-skin for my dress suit,
I thought me quite a beau,
When I was once a cave-boy,
A million years ago.

I dreamed I was a cave-boy;
My dinner was a bone,
And how I had to fight for it,
To get it for my own!
We banged each other o'er the head,
And oft our blood did glow,
When I was once a cave-boy,
A million years ago.

I dreamed I was a cave-boy.
The torches' smoky light
Shone on the dinner table,
A pile of bones so white.
I lapped some water from the spring,
The easiest way, you know,
When I was once a cave-boy,
A million years ago.

I dreamed – but now I am awake;
a voice is in my ear.
"Come out and have a game of ball!
The sun is shining clear.
We'll have some doughnuts afterwards,
And then a-swimming go!"
I'm glad I'm not a cave-boy,
A million years ago!

Laura E Richards

WENT TO THE RIVER

Went to the river, couldn't get across,

Paid five dollars for an old grey hoss.

Hoss wouldn't pull so I traded for a bull.

Bull wouldn't holler so I traded for a dollar.

Dollar wouldn't pass so I threw it on the grass.

Grass wouldn't grow so I traded for a hoe.

Hoe wouldn't dig so I traded for a pig.

Pig wouldn't squeal so I traded for a wheel.

Wheel wouldn't run so I traded for a gun.

Gun wouldn't shoot so I traded for a boot.

Boot wouldn't fit so I thought I'd better quit.

So I quit.

Anonymous

BALLOON

as
big   as
ball as round
as sun . . . I tug
and pull you when
you run and when
wind blows I
say polite
ly
H
O
L
D

M
E
T
I
G
H
T
L
Y.

Colleen Thibaudeau

THE OWL AND THE PUSSY-CAT

The Owl and the Pussy-cat went to sea
In a beautiful pea-green boat,
They took some honey, and plenty of money,
Wrapped up in a five-pound note.
The Owl looked up to the stars above,
And sang to a small guitar,
"O lovely Pussy! O Pussy, my love,
What a beautiful Pussy you are,
You are,
You are!
What a beautiful Pussy you are!"

Pussy said to the Owl, "You elegant fowl!
How charmingly sweet you sing!
Let us be married! Too long we have tarried:
But what shall we do for a ring?"
They sailed away, for a year and a day,
To the land where the Bong-tree grows
And there in a wood a Piggy-wig stood
With a ring at the end of his nose,
His nose,
His nose,
With a ring at the end of his nose.

"Dear Pig, are you willing to sell for one shilling
Your ring?" Said the Piggy, "I will."
So they took it away, and were married next day
By the Turkey who lives on the hill.
They dined on mince, and slices of quince,
Which they ate with a runcible spoon;
And hand in hand, on the edge of the sand,
They danced by the light of the moon,
The moon,
The moon,
They danced by the light of the moon.

Edward Lear

THE MAN IN THE MOON

The Man in the Moon
In a hot-air balloon
Came down to see the Queen.
But the Queen was away
For a year and a day,
Riding her sewing machine.

The Man in the Moon
Went round the world
And found the Queen in Spain.
So they flew the balloon
Back up to the moon,
And never came back again.

Georgie Adams

THE WHITE SHIPS

Out from the beach the ships I see
On cloudy sails move sleepily,
And though the wind be fair and strong
I watch them steal like ants along,
Following free, or wheeling now
To dip the sun a golden prow.

But when I ride upon the train
And turn to find the ships again,
I catch them far against the sky,
With crowded canvas hurrying by,
To all intent as fast as we
Are thundering beside the sea.

David McCord

FROM A RAILWAY CARRIAGE

Faster than fairies, faster than witches,

Bridges and houses, hedges and ditches;

And charging along like troops in a battle,

All through the meadows the horses and cattle:

All of the sights of the hill and the plain

Fly as thick as driving rain;

And ever again, in the wink of an eye,

Painted stations whistle by.

Here is a child who clambers and scrambles,

All by himself and gathering brambles;

Here is a tramp who stands and gazes;

And there is the green for stringing the daisies!

Here is a cart run away in the road

Lumping along with man and load;

And here is a mill and there is a river:

Each a glimpse and gone for ever!

Robert Louis Stevenson

THE WISE MEN OF GOTHAM

In a bowl to sea went wise men three,
    On a brilliant night of June:
They carried a net, and their hearts were set
    On fishing up the moon.

The sea was calm, the air was balm,
    Not a breath stirred low or high,
And the moon, I trow, lay as bright below,
    And as round as in the sky.

The wise men with the current went,
    Nor paddle nor oar had they,
And still as the grave they went on the wave,
    That they might not disturb their prey.

Far, far at sea were the wise men three,
    When their fishing net they threw;
And at their throw the moon below
    In a thousand fragments flew.

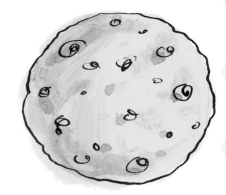

They drew in their net, it was empty and wet,
    And they had lost their pain,
Soon ceased the play of each dancing ray,
    And the image was round again.

Three times they threw, three times they drew,
    And all the while were mute;
And ever anew their wonder grew,
    Till they could not but dispute.

The three wise men got home again
    To their children and their wives:
But touching their trip and their net's vain dip
    They disputed all their lives.

The wise men three could never agree
    Why they missed their promised boon;
They agreed alone that their net they had thrown,
    And they had not caught the moon.

Thomas Love Peacock

I KNOW WHERE I'M GOING

I know where I'm going,
And I know who's going with me.
I know who I love,
But the dear knows who I'll marry.

I'll have stockings of silk,
Shoes of fine green leather,
Combs to buckle my hair
And a ring for every finger.

Feather beds are soft,
Painted rooms are bonny:
But I'd leave them all
To go with my Johnny.

Some say he's dark,
But I say he's bonny,
He's the flower of them all,
My handsome, winsome Johnny.

I know where I'm going,
And I know who's going with me.
I know who I love,
But the dear knows who I'll marry.

Anonymous

IF I SHOULD EVER BY CHANCE

If I should ever by chance grow rich
I'll buy Codham, Cockridden, and Childerditch,
Roses, Pyrgo, and Lapwater,
And let them all to my elder daughter.
The rent I shall ask of her will be only
Each year's first violets, white and lonely,
The first primroses and orchises –
She must find them before I do, that is.
But if she finds a blossom on furze
Without rent they shall all for ever be hers,
Whenever I am sufficiently rich:
Codham, Cockridden, and Childerditch,
Roses, Pyrgo and Lapwater –
I shall give them all to my elder daughter.

Edward Thomas

MY PLAN

When I'm a little older
I plan to buy a boat,
And up and down the river
The two of us will float.

I'll have a little cabin
All painted white and red
With shutters for the window
And curtains for the bed.

I'll have a little cookstove
On which to fry my fishes,
And all the Hudson River
In which to wash my dishes.

Marchette Chute

TARTARY

If I were Lord of Tartary,
Myself, and me alone,
My bed should be of ivory,
Of beaten gold my throne;
And in my court should peacocks flaunt,
And in my forests tigers haunt,
And in my pools great fishes slant
Their fins athwart the sun.
If I were Lord of Tartary,
Trumpeters every day
To all my meals should summon me,
And in my courtyards bray;
And in the evening lamps should shine,
Yellow as honey, red as wine,
While harp, and flute, and mandoline
Made music sweet and gay.
If I were Lord of Tartary,
I'd wear a robe of beads,
White, and gold, and green they'd be –
And small and thick as seeds;
And ere should wane the morning star,
I'd don my robe and scimitar,
And zebras seven should draw my car
Through Tartary's dark glades.

Lord of the fruits of Tartary,
Her rivers silver-pale!
Lord of the hills of Tartary,
Glen, thicket, wood, and dale!
Her flashing stars, her scented breeze,
Her trembling lakes, like foamless seas,
Her bird-delighting citron-trees,
In every purple vale!

Walter de la Mare

BUILDING A SKYSCRAPER

They're building a skyscraper
Near our street.
Its height will be nearly
One thousand feet.

It covers completely
A city block.
They drilled its foundation
Through solid rock.

They made its framework
Of great steel beams
With riveted joints
And welded seams.

A swarm of workmen
Strain and strive,
Like busy bees
In a honeyed hive.

Building a skyscraper
Into the air
While crowds of people
Stand and stare.

Higher and higher
The tall towers rise
Like Jacob's ladder
Into the skies.

James S Tippett

119

A TRAGIC STORY

There lived a sage in days of yore,
And he a handsome pigtail wore:
But wondered much, and sorrowed more,
    Because it hung behind him.

He mused upon this curious case,
And swore he'd change the pigtail's place,
And have it hanging at his face,
    Not dangling there behind him.

Says he, "The mystery I've found –
I'll turn me round," – he turned him round;
    But still it hung behind him.

Then round, and round, and out and in,
All day the puzzled sage did spin;
In vain – it mattered not a pin –
    The pigtail hung behind him.

And right and left, and round about,
And up and down, and in and out,
He turned; but still the pigtail stout
    Hung steadily behind him.

And though his efforts never slack,
And though he twist, and twirl, and tack,
Alas! still faithful to his back,
    The pigtail hangs behind him.

William Makepeace Thackeray

Rub-a-dub-dub,
Three men in a tub,
And how do you think they got there?
The butcher, the baker,
The candlestick-maker,
They all jumped out of a rotten potato,
T'was enough to make a man stare.

Traditional

THE LION AND THE UNICORN

The lion and the unicorn
Were fighting for the crown;
The lion beat the unicorn
All round the town.

Some gave them white bread,
And some gave them brown;
Some gave them plumcake,
And drummed them out of town.

Anonymous

QUICK!

Beg your pardon, Mrs Martin,
There's a piggy in your garden
And he's eaten all the cabbages
And beans.

So you'd better go and thump him
'Cause he's chewing up the pumpkin
And he's trampled on the radishes
And greens!

Anonymous

127

THE MOUSE'S TALE

Fury said to
a mouse, That
he met in the
house, "Let
us both go
to law: *I*
will prose-
cute *you.* -
Come, I'll
take no de-
nial: We
must have
the trial;
For really
this morn-
ing I've
nothing
to do."
Said the
mouse to
the cur,
"Such a
trial, dear
sir, With
no jury
or judge,
would
be wast-
ing our
breath."
"I'll be
judge,
I'll be
jury,"
said
cun-
ning
old
Fury:
"I'll
try
the
whole
cause,
and
con-
demn
you to
death."

Lewis Carroll

128

A CAT CAME DANCING OUT OF A BARN

A cat came dancing out of a barn
With a pair of bagpipes under her arm;
She could sing nothing but fiddle cum fee,
The mouse has married the bumblebee.
Pipe, cat; dance, mouse;
We'll have a wedding at our good house.

Traditional

FROG

A frog once went out walking,
In the pleasant summer air,
He happened into a barber's shop
And skipped into the chair.
The barber said in disbelief;
"Your brains are surely bare.
How can you have a haircut
When you haven't any hair?"

Anonymous

CATKIN

I have a little pussy
And her coat is silver grey;
She lives in a great wide meadow
And she never runs away.
She'll always be a pussy,
She'll never be a cat,
Because – she's a pussy willow!
Now what do you think of that?

Anonymous

FIVE LITTLE POSSUMS

Five little possums
Sat in a tree
The first one said,
"What do I see?"
The second one said,
"A man with a gun."
The third one said,
"We'd better run."
The fourth one said,
"Let's hide in the shade."
The fifth one said,
"I'm not afraid."

Then BANG went the gun
And how they did run!

Anonymous

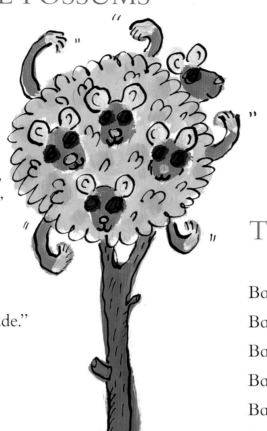

THE BAT

Bats are creepy; bats are scary;
Bats do not seem sanitary;
Bats in dismal caves keep cozy;
Bats remind us of Lugosi;
Bats have webby wings that fold up;
Bats from ceilings hang down rolled up;
Bats when flying undismayed are;
Bats are careful; bats use radar;
Bats at nighttime at their best are;
Bats by Batman unimpressed are!

Frank Jacobs

SCRATCH, SCRATCH!

I've got a dog as thin as a rail.
He's got fleas all over his tail;
Every time his tail goes flop,
The fleas at the bottom all hop to the top.

Anonymous

BESIDE THE LINE OF ELEPHANTS

I think they had no pattern
When they cut out the elephant's skin;
Some places it needs letting out,
And others, taking in.

Edna Becker

Donkey, donkey, old and grey,
Open your mouth, and gently bray;
Lift your ears and blow your horn,
To wake the world this sleepy morn.

Anonymous

RED FOX

On the stone ridge east I go.
On the white road I, red fox, crouching go.
I, red fox, whistle on the road of stars.

Wintu Traditional Song

131

AS I LOOKED OUT

As I looked out on Saturday last,

A fat little pig went hurrying past,

Over his shoulder he wore a shawl,

Although it didn't seem cold at all.

I waved at him, but he didn't see,

For he never so much as looked at me.

Once again, when the moon was high,

I saw the little pig hurrying by;

Back he came at a terrible pace,

The moonlight shone on his little pink face,

And he smiled with a smile that was quite content,

But I never knew where that little pig went.

Anonymous

IT IS I, THE LITTLE OWL

Who is it up there on top of the lodge?
Who is it up there on top of the lodge?
It is I,
The little owl,
coming down –
It is I,
The little owl,
coming down –
coming down –
down –
coming
down –
down –

Who is it whose eyes are shining up there?
Who is it whose eyes are shining up there?
It is I,
The little owl,
coming down –
It is I,
The little owl,
coming down –
coming –
down –
coming
down –
down –

Chippewa Indian

FIVE LITTLE OWLS

Five little owls in an old elm tree,
Fluffy and puffy as owls could be,
Blinking and winking with big round eyes
At the big round moon that hung in the skies.

Anonymous

THE GOAT

There was a man, now please take note,
There was a man, who had a goat,
He lov'd that goat, indeed he did,
He lov'd that goat, just like a kid.

One day that goat felt frisk and fine,
Ate three red shirts from off the line.
The man he grabbed him by the back,
And tied him to a railroad track.

But when the train hove into sight,
That goat grew pale and green with fright.
He heaved a sigh, as if in pain,
Coughed up those shirts and flagged the train.

Anonymous

AN AWFUL MOMENT

Soon as Caesar, our dog, spied that fox-fur scarf
He jumped to his feet and started in to arf

And the lady went Aaaggghhh! Why, he shot up and took it
Off from around her neck and just shook the thing and shook it.

Dad talked to him a long time. But me, I'm afraid he
Had better steer clear of that hopping mad lady.

She should keep her old scarf out of sight in a box.
Why does one skinny neck need a whole furry fox?

X J Kennedy

IF YOU SHOULD MEET A CROCODILE

If you should meet a crocodile,
Don't take a stick and poke him;
Ignore the welcome in his smile,
Be careful not to stroke him.
For as he sleeps upon the Nile,
He thinner gets and thinner;
And whene'er you meet a crocodile
He's ready for his dinner.

Anonymous

THE CATERPILLAR

Brown and furry
Caterpillar in a hurry,
Take your walk
To the shady leaf or stalk.

May no toad spy on you,
May the little birds pass by you.
Spin and die,
To live again a butterfly.

Christina Rossetti

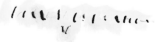

GROUNDHOG DAY

Groundhog sleeps
All winter
Snug in his fur,
Dreams
Green dreams of
Grassy shoots,
Of nicely newly nibbly
Roots –
Ah, he starts to
Stir.
With drowsy
Stare
Looks from his burrow
Out on fields of
Snow.
What's there?
Oh no.
His shadow. Oh,
How sad!
Six more
Wintry
Weeks
To go.

Lilian Moore

THE HAIRY DOG

My dog's so furry I've not seen
His face for years and years:
His eyes are buried out of sight,
I only guess his ears.

When people ask me for his breed,
I do not know or care:
He has the beauty of them all
Hidden beneath his hair.

Herbert Asquith

137

A FARMYARD SONG

I had a cat and the cat pleased me,
I fed my cat by yonder tree;
    Cat goes fiddle-i-fee.

I had a hen and the hen pleased me,
I fed my hen by yonder tree;
    Hen goes chimmy-chuck,
      chimmy-chuck,
    Cat goes fiddle-i-fee.

I had a duck and the duck pleased me,
I fed my duck by yonder tree;
    Duck goes quack, quack,
    Hen goes chimmy-chuck,
      chimmy-chuck,
    Cat goes fiddle-i-fee.

I had a goose and the goose pleased me,
I fed my goose by yonder tree;
    Goose goes swishy, swashy,
    Duck goes quack, quack,
    Hen goes chimmy-chuck,
      chimmy-chuck,
    Cat goes fiddle-i-fee.

I had a sheep and the sheep pleased me,
I fed my sheep by yonder tree;
    Sheep goes baa, baa,
    Goose goes swishy, swashy,
    Duck goes quack, quack,
    Hen goes chimmy-chuck,
      chimmy-chuck,
    Cat goes fiddle-i-fee.

I had a pig and the pig pleased me,
I fed my pig by yonder tree;
    Pig goes griffy, gruffy,
    Sheep goes baa, baa,
    Goose goes swishy, swashy,
    Duck goes quack, quack,
    Hen goes chimmy-chuck,
      chimmy-chuck,
    Cat goes fiddle-i-fee.

I had a cow and the cow pleased me,
I fed my cow by yonder tree;
    Cow goes moo, moo,
    Pig goes griffy, gruffy,
    Sheep goes baa, baa,
    Goose goes swishy, swashy,
    Duck goes quack, quack,
    Hen goes chimmy-chuck,
      chimmy-chuck,
    Cat goes fiddle-i-fee.

I had a horse and the horse pleased me,
I fed my horse by yonder tree;
    Horse goes neigh, neigh,
    Cow goes moo, moo,
    Pig goes griffy, gruffy,
    Sheet goes baa, baa,
    Goose goes swishy, swashy,
    Duck goes quack, quack,
    Hen goes chimmy-chuck,
      chummy-chuck,
    Cat goes fiddle-i-fee.

I had a dog and the dog pleased me,
I fed my dog by yonder tree;
    Dog goes bow-wow, bow-wow,
    Horse goes neigh, neigh,
    Cow goes moo, moo,
    Pig goes griffy, gruffy,
    Sheep goes baa, baa,
    Goose goes swishy, swashy,
    Duck goes quack, quack,
    Hen goes chimmy-chuck,
      chimmy-chuck,
    Cat goes fiddle-i-fee.

Traditional

BIRDS IN THE GARDEN

Greedy little sparrow,

Great big crow,

Saucy little tomtits

All in a row.

Are you very hungry,

No place to go?

Come and eat my breadcrumbs,

In the snow.

Anonymous

ENIGMA SARTORIAL

Consider the Penguin.

He's smart as can be –

Dressed in his dinner clothes

Permanently.

You never can tell,

When you see him about,

If he's just coming in

Or just going out!

Lucy W Rhu

SAUSAGE CAT

Behold the cat
the cat full of sausage
his ears do slope backwards
his coat's full of glossage

His whiskers extend
like happy antennae
he would count his blessings
but they are too many

He unfoldeth his limbs
he displayeth his fur
he narrows his eyes
and begins to purr

And his purring is smooth
as an old tree's mossage
Behold the cat
who is full of sausage.

Adrian Mitchell

MY CAT

My cat is asleep – white paws
folded under his chin
He is a soft grey
smudge on the round rug

Dozing in the sun
He is a warm round stone
with a fur collar

My cat is taking
a nap Not a whisker
trembles Not a hair
moves His breath goes
softly in and out

Stay in your holes mice!
My cat sees you
in his dreams
and he has left
his motor running!

Barbara Esbensen

143

GIRAFFE

How lucky
To live
So high
Above
The body,
Breathing
At heaven's
Level,
Looking
Sun
In the eye;
While down
Below

The neck's
Precarious
Stair,
Back, belly,
And legs
Take care
Of themselves,
Hardly
Aware
Of the head's
Airy
Affairs.

Valerie Worth

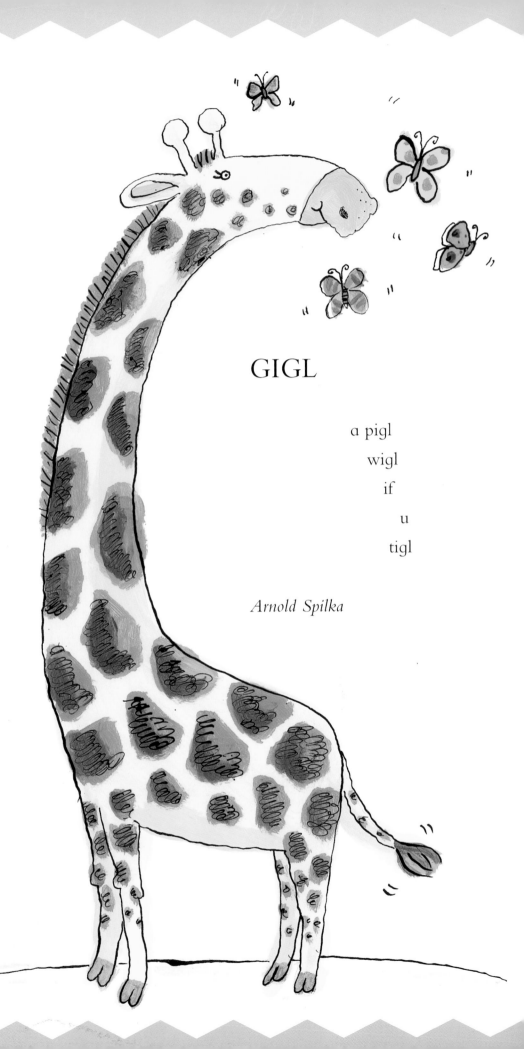

GIGL

a pigl
wigl
if
u
tigl

Arnold Spilka

144

SAID THE BOY TO THE DINOSAUR

Said the boy to the dinosaur:
"Outa my way!"
Said the dinosaur:
"That's not a nice thing to say."

Said the boy to the dinosaur:
"Go take a hike!"
Said the dinosaur:
"Not an expression I like."

Said the boy to the dinosaur:
"Move aside Mac!"
Said the dinosaur:
"Obviously, manners you lack."

Said the boy to the dinosaur:
"Go fly a kite!"
Said the dinosaur:
"That's what I call impolite."

Said the boy to the dinosaur:
"Jump in the lake!"
Said the dinosaur:
"That is as much as I'll take!"

The monster was cross,
Which is what you'd expect;
"I'm older than you,
You should show some respect!"

He taught him a lesson,
What more can I say?
The dinosaur ate him
And went on his way.

Colin McNaughton

145

HERE COME THE BEARS

Clambering through the rocky torrents
Here come the bears
Quicksilver salmon flip into the light
to flop a little higher up
swerving past scooping claws
and underwater gaping muzzles
to flip up into the light again
past the black tip
of the nose of a small bear
his eyes as wide as all amazement

Adrian Mitchell

MEASLES IN THE ARK

The night it was horribly dark,

The measles broke out in the Ark;

Little Japheth, and Shem, and all the young Hams,

Were screaming at once for potatoes and clams.

And "What shall I do," said poor Mrs Noah,

"All alone by myself in this terrible shower?

I know what I'll do: I'll step down in the hold,

And wake up a lioness grim and old,

And tie her close to the children's door,

And give her a ginger-cake to roar

At the top of her voice for an hour or more;

And I'll tell the children to cease their din,

Or I'll let that grim old party in,

To stop their squeazles and likewise their measles."

She practised this with the greatest success:

She was everyone's grandmother, I guess.

Susan Coolidge

SPEAKING OF COWS

Speaking of cows
(Which no one was doing)
Why are they always
Staring and chewing?
Staring at people,
Chewing at clover,
Doing the same things
Over and over.

Once in a while,
You see a cow mooing,
Swishing her tail
At a fly that needs shooing.

Most of the time, though,
What's a cow doing?
Munching and looking,
Staring and chewing.
Eyes never blinking,
Jaws always moving.
What are cows thinking?
What are cows proving?

Cows mustn't care for
New Ways of doing.
That's what they stare for;
That's why they're chewing.

Kaye Starbird

Little Tommy Tadpole began to weep and wail,
For little Tommy Tadpole had lost his little tail!
His mother did not know him as he sat upon a log,
For little Tommy Tadpole was now Mr Thomas Frog!

Anonymous

THAT CAT

The cat that comes to my window sill
When the moon looks cold and the night is still –
He comes in a frenzied state along
With a tail that stands like a pine tree cone.
And says: "I have finished my evening lark,
And I think I can hear a hound dog bark.
My whiskers are froze and stuck to my chin.
I do wish you'd git up and let me in."
That cat gits in.

But if in the solitude of the night
He doesn't appear to be feeling right,
And rises and stretches and seeks the floor,
And some remote corner he would explore,
And doesn't feel satisfied just because
There's no good spot for to sharpen his claws,
And meows and canters uneasy about
Beyond the least shadow of any doubt
That cat gits out.

Ben King

TWO NICE DOGS

Two little dogs went out for a walk,
    And it was windy weather,
So for fear the wind should blow them away,
    They tied their tails together.

They tied their tails with a yard of tape,
    And the wind it blew and blew,
As sharp and keen as a carving-knife,
    And cut the tape in two.

And away and away, like kites, in the air
    Those two little dogs flew about,
Till one little dog was blown to bits,
    And the other turned inside out.

Anonymous

The bear went over the mountain,
The bear went over the mountain,
The bear went over the mountain,
To see what he could see.

(And what do you think he saw?)
The other side of the mountain,
The other side of the mountain,
The other side of the mountain,
Was all that he could see.

So the bear went over the mountain,
The bear went over the mountain,
The bear went over the mountain,
So very happily.

Traditional

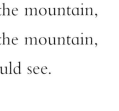

OUR HAMSTER'S LIFE

Our hamster's life:
there's not much
to it,
not much
to it.

He presses his pink nose
to the door of the cage
and decides for the fifty-six
millionth time
that he can't get
through it.

Our hamster's life:
there's not much
to it.

It's about the most boring
life in the world
if he only
knew it.
He sleeps and drinks and he eats.
He eats and he drinks and he sleeps.

He slinks and he dreeps.
He eats.

This process
he repeats.

Our hamster's life:
there's not much
to it,
not much
to it.

You'd think it would drive him bonkers,
going round and round on his wheel.
It's certainly driving me bonkers,

watching him
do it.

But he may be thinking:
"That boy's life,
there's not much
to it,
not much
to it:

watching a hamster go round on a wheel,
It's driving me bonkers if he only knew it,

watching him
watching me
do it."

Kit Wright

SONG OF THE RABBITS OUTSIDE THE TAVERN

We who play under the pines,
We who dance in the snow
That shines blue in the light of the moon
Sometimes halt as we go,
Stand with our ears erect,
Our noses testing the air,
To gaze at the golden world
Behind the windows there.

Suns they have in a cave
And stars each on a tall white stem,
And the thought of fox or night owl
Seems never to trouble them,
They laugh and eat and are warm,
Their food seems ready at hand,
While hungry out in the cold
We little rabbits stand.

But they never dance as we dance,
They have not the speed nor the grace.
We scorn both the cat and the dog
Who lie by their fireplace.
We scorn them licking their paws,
Their eyes on an upraised spoon,
We who dance hungry and wild
Under a winter's moon.

Elizabeth Coatsworth

Some people say that fleas are black,
But you know this isn't so,
For Mary had a little lamb
Whose fleas were white as snow.

Anonymous

POOR CROW!

Give me something to eat,
Good people, I pray;
I have really not had
One mouthful today!

I am hungry and cold,
And last night I dreamed
A scarecrow had caught me –
Good land, how I screamed!

Of one little children
And six ailing wives
(No, one wife and six children),
Not one of them thrives.

So pity my case,
Dear people, I pray;
I'm honest, and really
I've come a long way.

Mary Mapes Dodge

THE COMMON CORMORANT

The common cormorant or shag
Lays eggs inside a paper bag.
The reason you will see no doubt
It is to keep the lightning out.
But what these unobservant birds
Have never noticed is that herds
Of wandering bears may come with buns
And steal the bags to hold the crumbs.

Anonymous

155

AS I WAS STANDING IN THE STREET

As I was standing in the street,
As quiet as could be,
A great big ugly man came up
And tied his horse to me.

Anonymous

VERY POORLY

Two cats sat on a garden wall,
　　For an hour or so together;
At first they talked about nothing at all,
　　And then they talked of the weather.

The little pussycat, afraid of the cold,
　　Had a wrapper to wrap her chin in;
But the big pussycat, more silly than that,
　　Kept her tail in a bag of linen.

Said the little pussycat to the big pussycat,
　　"You've not very much to ail of;"
And so angry at that was the big pussycat,
　　That she bit the little one's tail off.

Anonymous

THE BOA

Allow me just one short remark
About this lengthy boa:
If Noah had it in his ark,
I sympathise with Noah!

J J Bell

THE SEA SERPANT
An Accurate Description

A-sleepin' at length on the sand,
Where the beach was all tidy and clean,
A-strokin' his scale with the brush on his tail
Thee wily Sea Serpant I seen.

And what was his colour? You asks,
And how did he look? Inquires you,
I'll be busted and blessed if he didn't look jest
Like you would of expected 'im to!

His head was the size of a – well,
The size what they always attains;
He whistled a tune what was built like a prune,
And his tail was the shape o' his brains.

His scales they was ruther – you know –
Like the leaves what you pick off o' eggs;
And the way o' his walk – well, it's useless to talk,
Fer o' course you've seen Sea Serpants' legs.

His length it was seventeen miles,
Or fathoms, or inches, or feet
(Me memory's sich that I can't recall which,
Though at figgers I've seldome been beat).

And I says as I looks at the beast,
"He reminds me o' somethin' I've seen –
Is it candy or cats or humans or hats,
Or Fenimore Cooper I mean?"

And as I debated the point,
In a way that I can't understand,
The Sea Serpant he disappeared in the sea
And walked through the ocean by land.

And somehow I knowed he'd come back,
So I marked off the place with me cap;
'Twas Latitude West and Longitude North
And forty-eight cents by the map.

And his length it was seventeen miles,
Or inches, or fathoms, or feet
(Me memory's sich that I can't recall which,
Though at figgers I've seldom been beat).

Wallace Irwin

157

LULLABY OF A DOG TO HER PUP

Here,
You like to be nursed in your young years,
You floppy thing.
Here,
You like to be nursed,
Little tail,
You wobbly one.

Crow Traditional Song

CATS

I don't go for prize cats
or oversize cats –
or for stuck-up bad-tempered
stuffy cats,
huffy cats,
or very very fluffy cats!
The Champion Persian
is not my favourite version.

I like ordinary cats,
even slightly shabby cats –
black, black-and-white, tortoiseshell, ginger
and tabby cats!

Gavin Ewart

LITTLE PIGGY

Where are you going, you little pig?

I'm leaving my mother, I'm growing so big!

So big, young pig!

So young, so big!

What, leaving your mother, you foolish young pig?

Where are you going, you little pig?

I've got a new spade, and I'm going to dig!

To dig, little pig!

A little pig dig!

Well, I never saw a pig with a spade that could dig!

Where are you going, you little pig?

Why, I'm going to have a nice ride in a gig!

In a gig, little pig!

What, a pig in a gig!

Well, I never yet saw a pig in a gig!

Where are you going, you little pig?

I'm going to the barber's to buy me a wig!

A wig, little pig!

A pig in a wig!

Why, whoever before saw a pig in a wig!

Where are you going, you little pig?

Why, I'm going to the ball to dance a fine jig!

A jig, little pig!

A pig dance a jig!

Well, I never before saw a pig dance a jig!

Thomas Hood

INCY WINCY SPIDER

Incy
Wincy
Spider
climbed the
water spout.
Down came
the rain
and washed
poor Incy
out.
Out came
the sun
and dried
up all
the rain.
And Incy
Wincy
Spider
climbed
the spout
again.

Anonymous

MAGGIE

There was a small maiden named Maggie,
Whose dog was enormous and shaggy;
The front end of him
Looked vicious and grim –
But the tail end was friendly and waggy.

Anonymous

162

NOT A WORD

They walked the lane together,
The sky was dotted with stars.
They reached the rails together,
He lifted up the bars.

She neither smiled nor thanked him,
Because she knew not how,
For he was only the farmer's boy
And she was the Jersey cow!

Anonymous

THE FROG

Be kind and tender to the Frog,
And do not call him names,
As "Slimy-skin", or "Polly-wog",
Or likewise "Uncle James",
Or "Gape-a-grin", or "Toad-gone-wrong",
Or "Billy Bandy-knees":
The frog is justly sensitive
To epithets like these.

No animal will more repay
A treatment kind and fair,
At least, so lonely people say
Who keep a frog (and by the way,
They are extremely rare).

Hilaire Belloc

They tell me an elephant never forgets,
And, of course, what they say may be so.
That's all very well, but how can they tell?
I mean, how can they possibly know?

Finola Akister

DOGS AND WEATHER

I'd like a different dog
For every kind of weather –
A narrow greyhound for a fog,
A wolfhound strange and white,
With a tail like a silver feather
To run with in the night,
When snow is still, and winter stars are bright.

In the fall I'd like to see
In answer to my whistle,
A golden spaniel look at me.
But best of all for rain
A terrier, hairy as a thistle,
To trot with fine disdain
Beside me down the soaked, sweet-smelling lane.

Winifred Welles

TO THE LADYBIRD

Ladybird! Ladybird! Fly away home;
The field-mouse is gone to her nest,
The daisies have shut up their sleepy red eyes,
And the birds and the bees are at rest.

Ladybird! Ladybird! Fly away home;
The glow-worm is lighting her lamp,
The dew's falling fast, and your fine speckled wings
Will flag with the close-clinging damp.

Ladybird! Ladybird! Fly away home;
The fairy-bells tinkle afar;
Make haste, or they'll catch you and harness you fast
With a cobweb to Oberon's car.

Vachel Lindsay

THE SHARK

A treacherous monster is the shark
He never makes the least remark.

And when he sees you on the sand,
He doesn't seem to want to land.

He watches you take off your clothes,
And not the least excitement shows.

His eyes do not grow bright or roll,
He has astounding self-control.

He waits till you are quite undressed,
And seems to take no interest.

And when towards the sea you leap,
He looks as if he were asleep.

But when you once get in his range,
His whole demeanour seems to change.

He throws his body right about,
And his true character comes out.

It's no use crying or appealing,
He seems to lose all decent feeling.

After this warning you will wish
To keep clear of this treacherous fish.

His back is black, his stomach white,
He has a very dangerous bite.

Lord Alfred Douglas

Oh where, oh where has my little dog gone,
Oh where, oh where can he be?
With his ears cut short and his tail cut long,
Oh where, oh where is he?

Anonymous

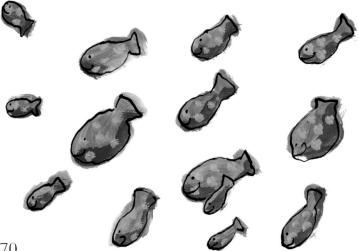

HOLDING
HANDS

Elephants walking
Along the trails

Are holding hands
By holding tails

Trunks and tails
Are handy things

When elephants walk
In circus rings.

Elephants work
And elephants play

And elephants walk
And feel so gay.

And when they walk –
It never fails

They're holding hands
By holding tails.

Lenore M Link

Hickory, dickory, dock!
The mouse ran up the clock,
The clock struck one,
Down the mouse ran,
Hickory, dickory, dock!

Hickory, dickory, dare!
The pig flew up in the air,
The man in brown
Soon brought him down,
Hickory, dickory, dare!

Anonymous

171

CHOOSING THEIR NAMES

Our old cat has kittens three –
What do you think their names should be?
One is tabby with emerald eyes,
And a tail that's long and slender,
And into a temper she quickly flies
If you ever by chance offend her.
I think we shall call her this –
I think we shall call her that –
Now, don't you think that Pepperpot
Is a nice name for a cat?
One is black with a frill of white,
And her feet are all white fur,
If you stroke her she carries her tail upright
And quickly begins to purr.
I think we shall call her this –
I think we shall call her that –
Now, don't you think that Sootikin
Is a nice name for a cat?
One is a tortoiseshell yellow and black,
With plenty of white about him;
If you tease him, at once he sets up his back,
He's a quarrelsome one, ne'er doubt him.
I think we shall call him this –
I think we shall call him that –

Now, don't you think that Scratchaway
Is a nice name for a cat?
Our old cat has kittens three
And I fancy these their names will be:
Pepperpot, Sootikin, Scratchaway – there!
Were ever kittens with these to compare?
And we call the old mother –
Now, what do you think? – Tabitha
Longclaws Tiddley Wink.

Thomas Hood

THE KANGAROO

Old Jumpety-Bumpety-Hop-and-Go-One
Was lying asleep on his side in the sun.
This old kangaroo, he was whisking the flies
(With his long glossy tail) from his ears and his eyes.
Jumpety-Bumpety-Hop-and-Go-One
Was lying asleep on his side in the sun.
Jumpety-Bumpety-Hop!

Traditional Australian

Whose little pigs are these, these, these?
Whose little pigs are these?
They're Roger the Cook's,
I know by their looks;
And I found them among my peas.
Go pound them, go pound them.
I dare not on my life,
For though I love not Roger,
I dearly love his wife.

Anonymous

HARE SONG

Hare is jumping and singing;
Hare is jumping and singing,
While the wind is roaring,
While the wind is roaring.

Hare is dancing and singing;
Hare is dancing and singing,
While the clouds are roaring,
While the clouds are roaring.

Traditional North American

LEOPARD IN THE ZOO

The lovely leopard
dreaming of
the dark jungle

and tangled vines,
monkeys and
hot moist days,

doesn't care
about children
who stare
wondering
what
he
dreams

Charlotte Zolotow

A POEM FOR MY CAT

You're black and sleek and beautiful
What a pity your best friends won't tell you
Your breath smells of Kit-E-Kat.

Adrian Henri

MARY'S LAMB

Mary had a little lamb,
Its fleece was white as snow,
And everywhere that Mary went
The lamb was sure to go;
He followed her to school one day –
That was against the rule,
It made the children laugh and play
To see a lamb at school.

Sarah Josepha Hale

WHAT REALLY HAPPENED

Humpty Dumpty
Sat in the corner
While Little Jack Horner
Sat on a wall
But Little Miss Muffet
Stayed on her tuffet,
Not being frightened
Of spiders at all

John Mole

When it was my birthday,
Daddy asked what I would choose
For a special birthday present,
So I answered, "Dancing shoes."

We went to town to buy some,
But they cost an awful lot.
"Have you any cheaper?" Daddy asked,
But that was all they'd got.

So Daddy had to pay the price,
Though he made an awful fuss.
"I'm glad you're a little girl," he said,
"And not an octopus."

Finola Akister

I AM RUNNING IN A CIRCLE

I am running in a circle
and my feet are getting sore,
and my head is
spinning
spinning
as it's never spun before,
I am
dizzy
dizzy
dizzy.
Oh! I cannot bear much more,
I am trapped in a
revolving
. . .volving
. . .volving
. . .volving door!

Jack Prelutsky

THE POSTMAN

The whistling postman swings along.
His bag is deep and wide,
And messages from all the world
Are bundled up inside.
The postman's walking up our street.
Soon now he'll ring my bell.
Perhaps there'll be a letter stamped
In Asia. Who can tell?

John Drinkwater

OLD JOE CLARKE

Old Joe Clarke, he had a house,
Was fifteen stories high,
And every darn room in that house
Was full of chicken pie.

I went down to Old Joe Clarke's
And found him eating supper;
I stubbed my toe on the table leg
And stuck my nose in the butter.

I went down to Old Joe Clarke's
But Old Joe wasn't in;
I sat right down on the red-hot stove
And got right up again.

Anonymous

TONY O

Over the bleak and barren snow
A voice there came a-calling;
"Where are you going to, Tony O?
Where are you going this morning?"

"I am going where there are rivers of wine,
The mountains bread and honey;
There kings and queens do mind the swine,
And the poor have all the money."

Anonymous

RUMBO AND JUMBO

Lord Rumbo was immensely rich
And he would stick at nothing.
He went about in golden boots
And silver underclothing.

Lord Jumbo, on the other hand,
Though mentally acuter,
Could only run to silver boots,
His underclothes were pewter.

Anonymous

MR NOBODY

I know a funny little man,
As quiet as a mouse,
Who does the mischief that is done
In everybody's house!
There's no one ever sees his face,
And yet we all agree
That every plate we break was cracked
By Mr Nobody.

'Tis he who always tears our books,
Who leaves the door ajar,
He pulls the buttons from our shirts,
And scatters pins afar;
That squeaking door will always squeak,
For, prithee, don't you see,
We leave the oiling to be done
By Mr Nobody.

The finger marks upon the door
By none of us are made;
We never leave the blinds unclosed,
To let the curtains fade.
The ink we never spill; the boots
That lying round you see
Are not our boots – they all belong
To Mr Nobody.

Robert Louis Stevenson

HERE LIES FRED

Here lies Fred,
Who was alive and is dead.
Had it been his father,
I had much rather;
Had it been his brother,
Still better than another;
Had it been his sister,
No one would have miss'd her;
Had it been the whole generation,
Still better for the nation;
But since 'tis only Fred,
Who was alive and is dead,
There's no more to be said.

Anonymous

After the ball was over,
She lay on the sofa and sighed.
She put her false teeth in salt water
And took out her lovely glass eye.
She kicked her wood leg in the corner,
Hung up her wig on the wall,
She closed her real eye and sang softly
"After the Ball."

Anonymous

179

DOWN BY THE RIVER

Down by the river,
Where the green grass grows
Little Polly Perkins washes her clothes.
She sings, she sings, she sings so sweet,
She calls to her playmates in the street.

Patrick, Patrick
Won't you come to tea?
Come next Saturday at half past three;
Tea cakes, pancakes, everything to see –
Oh won't we have a jolly time at half past three!

Anonymous

SCATTERBRAIN

Before he goes to bed at night
Scatterbrained Uncle Pat
Gives the clock a saucer of milk
And winds up the tabby cat.

Gareth Owen

There is one thing I cannot do
Because, you see, I'm only two.
No matter how I try and try,
It nearly always makes me cry.
I don't know when it all began,
Or why some very clever man
Thought that buttons could be fun –
I simply can't get mine undone.
My mother comes and helps me out,
But, really, what's it all about?
Although I try, it's all in vain.
I just can't do them up again.

Finola Akister

MY FRONT TOOTH

When my front tooth came out,
Miss wrapped it in tissue paper
And looked after it for me
Until hometime.

When I got home,
I took it out and put it down
On the carpet to examine it.
Just then, Samson, our dog
Came bounding in.
Before I could stop him,
He'd gobbled up the tooth
And swallowed it.

"Serves you right
For not looking after it properly,"
Said my sister.
"Now you won't get anything
From the tooth fairy."

"I will, won't I, Mum?" I said,
But all she said was,
"Wait and see."

That night,
I put a note under my pillow
Explaining what had happened.

In the morning, it had gone.
But there was no sign
Of any money.

Feeling fed up, I went downstairs
To let Samson out,
Propped against his basket
Was an envelope addressed to
The Owner of the Lost Tooth.

I tore it open.
Inside there was a note
From the tooth fairy, which said:
Although your tooth cannot be found,
The dog's to blame,
So here's your pound.

John Foster

BATH

Wash wash in the bath
even though I'm not dirty.
If I keep on washing every day
I'll be clean by the time I'm thirty.

Pauline Stewart

CORAL

"O sailor, come ashore,
What have you brought for me?"
"Red coral, white coral,
Coral from the sea.
I did not dig it from the ground,
Nor pluck it from the tree;
Feeble insects made it
In the stormy sea."

Christina Rossetti

AUNTY AGGIE

Cleaning round the house one day,
Aunty Aggie went astray;
Sucked up by the vacuum cleaner,
Since which time, no-one has seen her.
Where she is, there's just no knowing,
But when the thing was overflowing,
It seems to me without a doubt,
They simply threw the old bag out.

Mike Jubb

184

THERE WAS AN OLD MAN OF BLACKHEATH

There was an old man of Blackheath,
Who sat on his set of false teeth.
Said he, with a start,
"O Lord, bless my heart!
I've bitten myself underneath!"

Anonymous

THE DAUGHTER
OF THE FARRIER

The daughter of the farrier
Could find no one to marry her,
Because she said
She would not wed
A man who could not carry her.

The foolish girl was wrong enough,
And had to wait quite long enough;
For as she sat
She grew so fat
That nobody was strong enough.

Anonymous

GROWING UP

When I was seven
We went for a picnic
Up to a magic
Foresty place.
I knew there were tigers
Behind every boulder,
Though I didn't meet one
Face to face.

When I was older
We went for a picnic
Up to the very same
Place as before,
And all of the trees
And the rocks were so little
They couldn't hide tigers
Or me any more.

Harry Behn

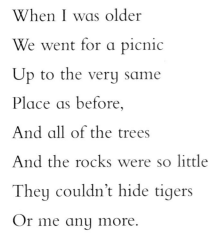

Anna Elise, she jumped with surprise.

The surprise was so quick,

It played her a trick.

The trick was so rare,

She jumped in a chair.

The chair was so frail,

She jumped in a pail.

The pail was so wet,

She jumped in a net.

The net was so small,

She jumped on a ball.

The ball was so round,

She jumped on the ground.

And ever since then

She's been turning around.

Anonymous

Sukey, you shall be my wife,
And I will tell you why:
I have got a little pig,
And you have got a sty;
I have got a dun cow,
And you can make good cheese;
Sukey, will you have me?
Say "yes," if you please.

Traditional

I'M A NAVVY

I'm a navvy, you're a navvy,
Working on the line,
Five-and-twenty bob a week
And all the overtime.
Roast beef, boiled beef,
Puddings made of eggs,
Up jumps a navvy
With a pair of sausage legs!

Anonymous

SIMPLE SIMON

Simple Simon went a-fishing
For to catch a whale;
All the water he had got
Was in his mother's pail.

Simple Simon went a-skating
On a pond in June.
"Dear me," he cried, "this water's wet,
I fear I've come too soon!"

Simple Simon made a snowball,
And brought it home to roast;
He laid it down before the fire,
And soon the ball was lost.

Anonymous

BOYS AND GIRLS COME OUT TO PLAY

Boys and girls, come out to play,

The moon doth shine as bright as day,

Leave your supper and leave your sleep,

And come with your playfellows into the street.

Come with a whoop or come with a call,

Come with a good will or not at all.

Up the ladder and down the wall,

A halfpenny roll will serve us all.

You find milk and I'll find flour,

And we'll have a pudding in half an hour!

Anonymous

MY BANGALOREY MAN

Follow my Bangalorey Man;

Follow my Bangalorey Man;

I'll do all that ever I can

To follow my Bangalorey Man.

We'll borrow a horse and steal a gig,

And round the world we'll do a jig,

And I'll do all that ever I can

To follow my Bangalorey Man.

Anonymous

DOWN IN YONDER MEADOW

Down in yonder meadow where the green grass grows,
Pretty Pollie Pillicote bleaches her clothes;.
She sang, she sang, she sang, oh, so sweet,
She sang, Oh, come over! across the street.

He kissed her, he kissed her, h\e bought her a gown,
A gown of rich crimson out of the town.
He bought her a gown and a guinea gold ring,
A guinea, a guinea, a guinea gold ring.

Up street, and down, shine the windows made of glass,
Oh, isn't Pollie Pillicote a braw young lass?
Cherries in her cheeks and ringlets in her hair,
Hear her singing Handy Dandy up and down the stair.

Anonymous

189

THE GIRL OF NEW YORK

There once was a girl of New York
Whose body was lighter than cork;
She had to be fed
For six weeks upon lead
Before she went out for a walk.

Cosmo Monkhouse

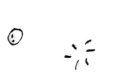

Miss Lucy had a baby,
She named him Tiny Tim,
She put him in the bathtub
To see if he could swim.

He drank up all the water,
He ate a bar of soap,
He tried to eat the bathtub,
But it wouldn't go down his throat.

Miss Lucy called the doctor,
Miss Lucy called the nurse,
Miss Lucy called the lady
With the alligator purse.

"Mumps," said the doctor,
"Measles," said the nurse,
"Chickenpox," said the lady
With the alligator purse.

Anonymous

DAME TROTTYPEG

In London-town Dame Trottypeg
   Lived high up in a garret;
And with her lived a wee pet dog,
   A tomcat and a parrot.

A cleverer or a funnier dog
   I'm sure you never saw;
For, like a sailor, he could dance
   A hornpipe on one paw.

And all the while the doggie danced,
   That pussy-cat was able
Just like a flute to play his tail
   Upon the kitchen table.

Anonymous

JEREMIAH OBADIAH

Jeremiah Obadiah
puff, puff, puff.
When he gives his messages he
snuffs, snuffs, snuffs,
When he goes to school by day he
roars, roars, roars,
When he goes to bed at night he
snores, snores, snores,
When he goes to Christmas treat he
eats plum-duff,
Jeremiah Obadiah
puff, puff, puff.

Anonymous

MY SHADOW

I have a little shadow that goes in and out with me,
And what can be the use of him is more than I can see.
He is very, very like me from the heels up to the head;
And I see him jump before me, when I jump into my bed.

The funniest thing about him is the way he likes to grow –
Not at all like proper children, which is always very slow;
For he sometimes shoots up taller like an India-rubber ball,
And he sometimes gets so little that there's none of him at all.

He hasn't got a notion of how children ought to play,
And can only make a fool of me in every sort of way.
He stays so close beside me, he's a coward you can see;
I'd think shame to stick to nursie as that shadow sticks to me!

One morning, very early, before the sun was up,
I rose and found the shining dew on every buttercup;
But my lazy little shadow, like an arrant sleepyhead,
Had stayed at home behind me and was fast asleep in bed.

Robert Louis Stevenson

HANK

HANK
Thin
as a
bean
pole,
wiry
as a
reed,
Hank
grew
fast
as a
must
-ard
seed,
tall
as a
lamp
post
with
long
flat
feet,
they
call
him Lanky Hanky
down   our   street.

Cynthia Mitchell

ALL ABOUT ME

I've got . . .

A head for nodding, shaking and thinking,
Eyes for seeing, closing and blinking.

Ears for hearing nice things and boring,
A nose for smelling, blowing and snoring.

A mouth for speaking, eating and kissing,
Teeth for chewing – my front tooth is missing.

Arms for waving, hugging and squeezing,
Hands for clapping, helping and pleasing.

Elbows and knees for bending and stretching,
Legs for kicking, running and fetching.

And right at the bottom my two little feet
For dancing and tapping a musical beat.

Georgie Adams

CRYING JACK

Once a little boy, Jack, was oh! Ever so good,
Till he took a strange notion to cry all he could.

So he cried all the day, and he cried all the night,
He cried in the morning and in the twilight;

He cried till his voice was as hoarse as a crow,
And his mouth grew so large it looked like a great O.

It grew at the bottom and grew at the top;
It grew till they thought that it never would stop.

Each day his great mouth grew taller and taller,
And his dear little self grew smaller and smaller.

At last, that same mouth grew so big that – alack! –
It was only a mouth with a border of Jack.

Anonymous

A barefoot boy with shoes on
Came shuffling down the street,
His pants were full of pockets,
His shoes were full of feet.

He was born when just a baby,
His mother's pride and joy,
His only sister was a girl,
His brother was a boy.

He never was a triplet,
He never was a twin,
His legs were fastened to his knees
Just above the shin.

His teeth were fastened in his head
Several inches from his shoulder.
When he grew up he became a man
And every day grew older.

Anonymous

LAURA

Laura's new this year in school.
She acts so opposite, it seems like a rule.
If someone says yes, Laura says no.
If someone says high, Laura says low.
If you say bottom, she'll say top.
If you say go, she'll say stop.
If you say short, Laura says tall.
If you say none, she says all.
If you say beginning, Laura says end . . .
but today she asked me to be her friend.
I said maybe
but not quite yes.
Then I said, "Want to take a walk?"
And Laura said, "I guess."

Jeff Moss

KING ARTHUR

When Good King Arthur ruled the land,
He was a goodly king;
He stole three sacks of barley meal
To make a bag-pudding.

A bag-pudding the Queen did bake,
And stuffed it full of plums,
And in it put great lumps of fat
As big as my two thumbs.

The King and Queen sat down to dine,
And all the court beside;
And what they could not eat that night
The Queen next morning fried.

Anonymous

DR FOSTER

Doctor Foster is a good man,
He teaches children all he can:
Reading, writing, arithmetic,
And doesn't forget to use his stick.
When he does he makes them dance
Out of England into France,
Out of France into Spain,
Round the world and back again.

Anonymous

TOM THUMB'S EPITAPH

Here lies Tom Thumb, King Arthur's Knight,
Who died by a spider's cruel bite.
He was well known in Arthur's court,
Where he afforded gallant sport.
He rode at tilt and tournament,
And on a mouse a-hunting went.
Alive he filled the court with mirth;
His death to sorrow soon gave birth.
Wipe, wipe your eyes and shake your head
And cry, – Alas! Tom Thumb is dead.

Anonymous

THERE WAS A LADY

There was a lady all skin and bone,
The skinniest lady ever known.
It happened on a certain day
The lady went to church to pray.

When she came to the church stile
She rested for a little while.
When she came to the churchyard,
There the ringing bells she heard.

When she came to the church door,
She stopped to rest a little more.
When at last she went inside,
The parson preached on sin and pride.

She looked up, and she looked down
And saw a skeleton on the ground.
In the body skull, on its bony chin
The worms crawled out, the worms crawled in.

Then she to the parson said,
Will I be a skeleton when I'm dead?
Oh, yes, oh, yes, the parson said,
You'll be like that when you are dead.

Anonymous

MY FACE

My face isn't pretty,
Nor is it quite plain –
I suppose it's an ordin'ry
Face in the main.

My mum says, "If even
You had your hair curled,
You wouldn't exactly
Be a Miss World,

But cheer up, my lovely,
Don't look glum all the while –
You'd look so much nicer
If only you'd smile!"

Anonymous

MY MOTHER SAID

My mother said I never should
Play with the gypsies in the wood;
If I did, she would say,
Naughty girl to disobey.
Your hair shan't curl
And your shoes shan't shine,
You gypsy girl,
You shan't be mine.

And my father said that if I did
He'd rap my head with the teapot lid.
The wood was dark; the grass was green;
In came Sally with a tambourine.
I went to the sea – no ship to get across;
I paid ten shillings for a blind white horse;
I up on his back and was off in a crack,
Sally tell my mother I shall never come back.

Anonymous

TOFFEE POCKETS

Grandad picks me up from school
With toffees by the pocketful
And all the children follow us
Home,
I wish I didn't have to share
The toffees that he keeps in there,
Why can't they get some grandads
Of their own?

Jeanne Willis

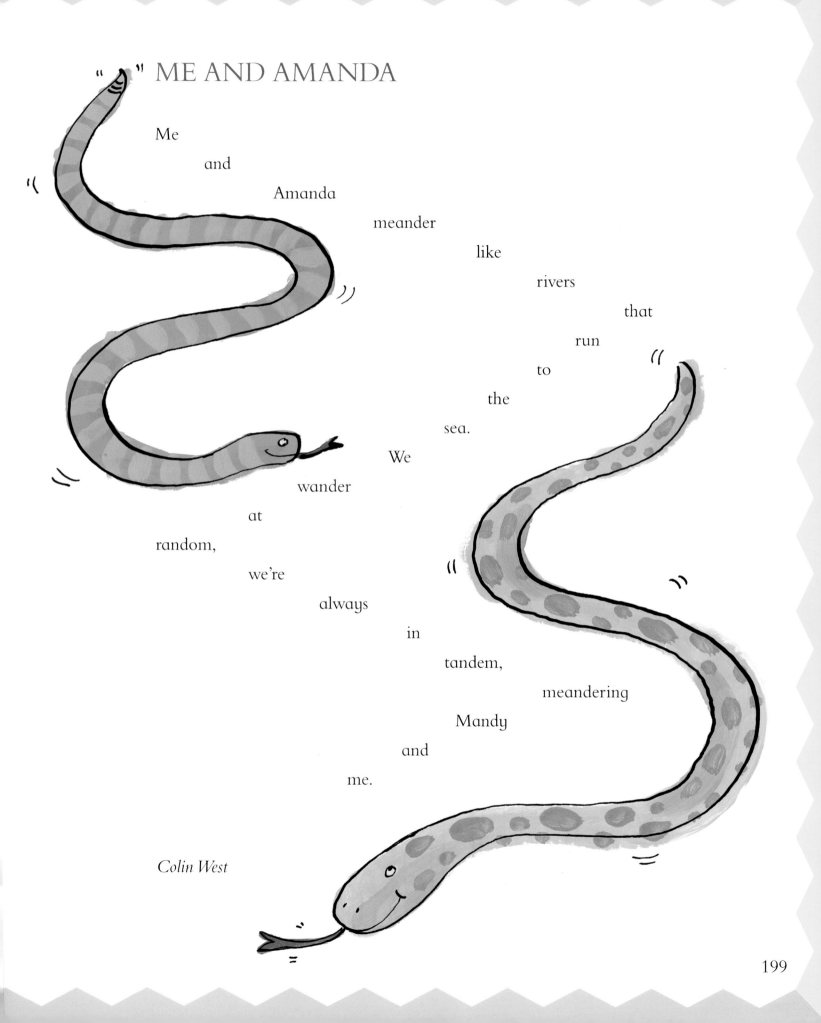

ME AND AMANDA

Me

and

Amanda

meander

like

rivers

that

run

to

the

sea.

We

wander

at

random,

we're

always

in

tandem,

meandering

Mandy

and

me.

Colin West

AT CHRISTMAS

I wish you a Merry Christmas,
I wish you a Merry Christmas,
I wish you a Merry Christmas
And a Happy New Year.

Good tidings I bring
To you and your kin;
I wish you a Merry Christmas
And a Happy New Year.

Now bring us some figgy pudding,
Now bring us some figgy pudding,
Now bring us some figgy pudding,
And bring some out here.

For we all like figgy pudding,
We all like figgy pudding,
For we all like figgy pudding,
So bring some out here.

And we won't go till we've got some,
And we won't go till we've got some,
And we won't go till we've got some,
So bring some out here.

Good tidings I bring
To you and your kin;
I wish you a Merry Christmas
And a Happy New Year.

Anonymous

CHRISTMAS IN THE SUN

I like when Christmas time is here
I like to welcome the New Year
I like the pretty coloured lights
hung outside on Christmas night.
This year,
I hope Santa will make a mistake
and shower us all in cool snowflakes.

Pauline Stewart

LONG, LONG AGO

Winds through the olive trees
Softly did blow,
Round little Bethlehem
Long, long ago.

Sheep on the hillside lay
Whiter than snow;
Shepherds were watching them,
Long, long ago.

Then from the happy sky,
Angels bent low,
Singing their songs of joy,
Long, long ago.

For in a manger bed,
Cradles we know,
Christ came to Bethlehem,
Long, long ago.

Anonymous

A NEW YEAR CAROL

Here we bring you new water from the well so clear,

For to worship God with this happy New Year.

Sing levy dew, the water and the wine;

The seven bright gold wires

And the bugles that do shine.

Sing reign of Fair Maid, with gold upon her toe,

Open you the West Door and turn the Old Year go.

Sing levy dew, the water and the wine;

The seven bright gold wires

And the bugles that do shine.

Sing reign of Fair Maid, with gold upon her chin,

Open you the East Door and let the New Year in.

Sing levy dew, the water and the wine;

The seven bright gold wires

And the bugles that do shine.

Anonymous

TROUBLE WITH PIES

Tomorrow's Christmas Day: three kinds of pies –
apple, mince, and pumpkin – all same size,
though not much bigger round than hungry eyes.

Since my first try at pie, I cannot choose
between mince, apple, pumpkin; or refuse
one, taking two of all those three good twos.

Apple and mince? Apple and pumpkin? What?
Leave pumpkin out, or mince? Well I guess not!
Pumpkin and mince? No apple have I got.

It would be better – best – to take all three;
but somehow that's not what they say to me.
"Which do you want?" they say. I say, "Let's see . . ."

David McCord

THE FRIENDLY BEASTS

Jesus our brother, kind and good,
Was humbly born in a stable rude;
The friendly beasts around Him stood,
Jesus our brother, kind and good.

"I," said the donkey, shaggy and brown,
"I carried His Mother up hill and down;
I carried her safely to Bethlehem town,
I," said the donkey, shaggy and brown.

"I," said the cow, all white and red,
"I gave Him my manger for His bed;
I gave Him my hay to pillow His head.
I," said the cow, all white and red.

"I," said the sheep with the curly horn,
"I gave Him my wool for a blanket warm.
He wore my coat on Christmas morn.
I," said the sheep with the curly horn.

"I," said the dove from the rafters high,
"I cooed Him to sleep so He would not cry,
I cooed Him to sleep, my mate and I.
I," said the dove from the rafters high.

And every beast, by some good spell,
In the stable dark was glad to tell,
Of the gift he gave Immanuel,
The gift he gave Immanuel.

Traditional

206

THE KING OF CHINA'S DAUGHTER

The King of China's daughter,
She never would love me,
Though I hung my cap and bells upon
Her nutmeg tree.
For oranges and lemons,
The stars in bright blue air
(I stole them long ago, my dear)
Were dangling there.
The Moon did give me silver pence,
The Sun did give me gold,
And both together softly blew
And made my porridge cold;
But the King of China's daughter
Pretended not to see
When I hung my cap and bells upon
The nutmeg tree.

The King of China's daughter
So beautiful to see
With her face like yellow water, left
Her nutmeg tree.
Her little rope for skipping
She kissed and gave it me –
Made of painted notes of singing-birds
Among the fields of tea.
I skipped across the nutmeg grove,
I skipped across the sea;
But neither sun nor moon, my dear,
Has yet caught me.

Edith Sitwell

207

NIGHT WALK

What are you doing away up there
On your great long legs in the lonely air?
    Come down here, where the scents are sweet,
    Swirling around your great, wide feet.

How can you know of the urgent grass
And the whiff of the wind that will whisper and pass
    Or the lure of the dark of the garden hedge
    Or the trail of a cat on the road's black edge?

What are you doing away up there
On your great long legs in the lonely air?
    You miss so much at your great, great height
    When the ground is full of the smells of night.

Hurry then, quickly, and slacken my lead
For the mysteries speak and the messages speed
    With the talking stick and the stone's slow mirth
    That four feet find on the secret earth.

Max Fatchen

THE DOOR

Why is there more
behind a door
than there is
before:
kings,
things
in store:
faces,
places
to explore:
The marvellous shore
the rolling floor,
the green man
by the sycamore

David McCord

208

SIMPLE GIFTS

'Tis the gift to be simple,
'Tis the gift to be free,
'Tis the gift to come down
Where we ought to be,
And when we find ourselves
In the place just right,
'Twill be in the valley
Of love and delight.
When true simplicity is gained,
To bow and to bend
We shan't be ashamed,
To turn, turn will be our delight,
Till by turning, turning
We come round right.

Anonymous Shaker Song

THE SECRET SONG

Who saw the petals
drop from the rose?
"I," said the spider,
But nobody knows.

Who saw the sunset
flash on a bird?
"I," said the fish,
But nobody heard.

Who saw the fog
come over the sea?
"I," said the sea-pigeon,
"Only me."

Who saw the first
green light of the sun?
"I," said the night owl,
The only one.

Who saw the moss
creep over the stone?
"I," said the grey fox,
All alone.

Margaret Wise Brown

THE SLEEPY GIANT

My age is three hundred and seventy-two,
And I think, with the deepest regret,
How I used to pick up and voraciously chew
The dear little boys whom I met.

I've eaten them raw, in their holiday suits;
I've eaten them curried with rice;
I've eaten them baked, in their jackets and boots,
And found them exceedingly nice.

But now that my jaws are too weak for such fare,
I think it exceedingly rude
To do such a thing, when I'm quite well aware
Little boys do not like to be chewed.

And so I contentedly live upon eels,
And try to do nothing amiss,
And I pass all the time I can spare from my meals
In innocent slumber – like this.

Charles E Carryl

212

THE GARDEN'S FULL OF WITCHES

Mum! The garden's full of witches!
Come quick and see the witches.
There's a full moon out,
And they're flying about,
Come on! You'll miss the witches.

Oh Mum! You're missing the witches.
You have never seen so many witches.
They are casting spells!
There are horrible smells!
Come on! You'll miss the witches.

Mum, hurry! Come look at the witches.
The shrubbery's bursting with witches.
They've turned our Joan
Into a garden gnome.
Come on! You'll miss the witches.

Oh no! You'll miss the witches.
The garden's black with witches.
Come on! Come on!
Too late! They've gone.
Oh, you always miss the witches!

Colin McNaughton

WHAT TO DO WHEN YOU MEET A GIANT

Don't shout out Wow! then stand and stare
Don't try to sit upon his chair
Don't ask him if it's cold up there
Don't ask if he liked Giant Despair
In John Bunyan's Pilgrim's Progress
Don't use the words Ogre or Ogress
Don't ask him if he'd like a snack
Or mention Beanstalks, David, Jack
Or even Snow White and the Seven –
Or say "You're very near to heaven"
Just be yourself and, in the end,
You may have made your greatest friend.

Adrian Mitchell

THE MAN WHO HID HIS OWN FRONT DOOR

There was a little, Elvish man
Who lived beside a moor,
A shy, secretive, furtive soul
Who hid his own front door.

He went and hid his door beneath
A pink laburnum bush:
The neighbours saw the curtains blow,
They heard a singing thrush.

The Banker came and jingled gold,
It did not serve him there;
The honey-coloured walls uprose
Unbroken and foursquare.

The Mayor called, the Misses Pitt
With cordials and game pie;
There was not any door at all,
They had to pass him by!

But ah! My little sister.
Her eyes were wild and sweet,
She wore blue faded calico,
And no shoes on her feet.

She found the wandering door in place
And easily went through
Into a strange and mossy Hall
Where bowls of old Delft blue

Held feasts of blackberries, like gems
In webs of shining dew –
There stood that little Elvish man
And smiled to see her, too!

Elizabeth MacKinstry

214

GREEN CANDLES

"There's someone at the door," said gold candlestick:
"Let her in quick, let her in quick!"
"There is a small hand groping at the handle.
Why don't you turn it?" asked green candle.

"Don't go, don't go," said the Hepplewhite chair,
"Lest you find a strange lady there."
"Yes, stay where you are," whispered the white wall:
"There is nobody there at all."

"I know her little foot," grey carpet said
"Who but I should know her light tread?"
"She shall come in," answered the open door,
"And not," said the room, "go out anymore."

Humbert Wolfe

THE DRAGON ON THE WALL

A bright green dragon comes in at the door
And crawls along the classroom wall.
He must be lost
Or need a rest
For he never came into the classroom before.

His body is hard as a fist with nobbly scales.
He could pull down a tree that he hooked with his tail.
He rests on the wall, his mouth open wide,
Puffing and panting flames from inside.

His green silky wings are raised on his back,
Ready to come down in one big flap
To carry him out of the open window
When no one's there to see him go.

When we leave him on his own
Does he fly home
In a streak of light
Through the black of the night
To see that his cave is safe
With all its bright shining gold?

Stanley Cook

On the mountain is a woman,
But who she is I do not know.
On her head are golden ribbons
And her hair is white as snow.

Anonymous

MARS

And then in my dream I slipped away
To the silver ship in the dawn of day,
To the grasshopper men with their queer green eyes
And suits that glittered in splendid dyes.
They came, they said, from a thirsty land,
A land that was dead and choked with sand;
The wells were empty and dusty and dry,
And the burning sun hung low in the sky;
"We are old," they said. "We have had our day,
And the silent cities crumble away."
"Yet here," they said, "we may find again
All that was carefree and lovely then
When the wells were full and the cities rang
With the harvest song that the reapers sang!"

. . . .

Oh, when I'm a man I shall travel to Mars
In a silver ship, in a night of stars,
And there I shall see those grasshopper men.
Without any doubt I shall know them again.

Anonymous

WHERE CAN IT BE?

A

long

time ago

there lived

a very old and

absent-minded

magician who was

always losing things,

especially his favourite hat.

Mike Jubb

181

STOCKING FAIRY

In a hole of the heel of an old brown stocking,

A little old Fairy sits rocking and rocking,

And scolding and pointing and squeaking and squinting,

Brown as a nut, a bright eye glinting,

She tugs at a thread, she drags up a needle,

She stamps and she shrills, she commences to wheedle,

To whine of the cold, in a fine gust of temper

She beats on my thumb, and then with a whimper

She sulks in her shawl, she says I've forgotten

I promised to make her a lattice of cotton,

A soft, woven window, cosy yet airy,

Where she could sit rocking and peeking – Hush, Fairy,

Tush, Fairy, sit gently, look sweetly,

I'll do what I said, now, and close you in neatly.

Winifred Welles

ROMANCE

I will make you brooches and toys for your delight
Of birdsong at morning and star shine at night.
I will make a palace fit for you and me,
Of green days in forests and blue days at sea.

I will make my kitchen, and you shall keep your room,
Where white flows the river and bright blows the broom,
And you shall wash your linen and keep your body white
In rainfall at morning and dewfall at night.

And this shall be for music, when no one else is near,
The fine song for singing, the rare song to hear!
That only I remember, that only you admire,
Of the broad road that stretches and the roadside fire.

Robert Louis Stevenson

WHEN I GROW UP

When I grow up,
I think I'll be
A detective
With a skeleton key.

I could be a soldier
And a sailor too;
I'd like to be a keeper
At the public zoo.

I'll own a trumpet
And I'll play a tune;
I'll keep a spaceship
To explore the moon.

I'll be a cowboy
And live in the saddle;
I'll be a guide
With a canoe and a paddle.

I'd like to be the driver
On a diesel train;
And it must be fun
To run a building crane.

I'll live in a lighthouse
And guard the shore;
And I know I'll want to be
A dozen things more.

For the more a boy lives
The more a boy learns –
I think I'll be all of them
By taking turns.

William Wise

THREE LITTLE GHOSTESSES

Three little ghostesses,
Sitting on postesses,
Eating buttered toastesses,
Greasing their fistesses,
Up to the wristesses,
Oh, what beastesses
To make such feastesses!

Anonymous

MAGIC CARPET

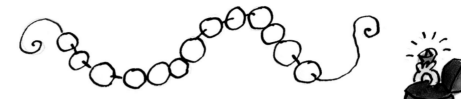

Magic carpet,
your bright colours
delight the eye.

Your moons and stars
and midnight blues
sing of the sky.

Magic carpet,
kept in the cupboard,
I hear you sigh.

Let me unroll
your magic pattern
and help you fly.

Tony Mitton

What do you choose?
Coral beads on a string,
Purple velvet and lace
And an emerald ring.

What will you have?
Pomegranates and pears,
Jellies, trifles and truffles
And chocolate eclairs.

What would you like?
A brown pony to ride
And three tiger-striped cats
To sleep at my side.

What is for you?
A palace fit for kings
With a grove of silver trees
Where a golden bird sings.

What is your wish?
To live by a storm tossed sea
In a lone grey tower
And hear the waves roaring
hungrily.

Olive Dove

GOLD AND LOVE FOR DEARIE

Out on the mountain over the town,
All night long, all night long,
The trolls go up and the trolls go down,
Bearing their packs and singing a song;
And this is the song the hill-folk croon,
As they trudge in the light of the misty moon –
This is ever their dolorous tune:
"Gold, gold! Ever more gold –
Bright red gold for dearie!"

Deep in the hill a father delves
All night long, all night long;
None but the peering, furtive elves
Sees his toil and hears his song;
Merrily ever the cavern rings
As merrily ever his pick he swings,
And merrily ever this song he sings:
"Gold, gold! Ever more gold –
Bright red gold for dearie!"

Mother is rocking thy lowly bed
All night long, all night long,
Happy to smooth thy curly head,
To hold thy hand and to sing her song:
'Tis not of the hill-folk dwarfed and old,
Nor the song of thy father, staunch and bold,
And the burthen it beareth is not of gold;
But it's "Love, love! Nothing but love –
Mother's love for dearie!"

Eugene Field

THE DRAGON OF WANTLEY

This dragon had two furious wings
One upon each shoulder,
With a sting in his tail as long as a flail
Which made him bolder and bolder.
He had long claws, and in his jaws
Four and forty teeth of iron,
With a hide as tough as any buff
Which did him round environ.

Have you not heard how the Trojan horse
Held seventy men in his belly?
This dragon wasn't quite so big
But very near I'll tell ye.
Devoured he poor children three
That could not with him grapple,
And at one sup he ate them up
As you would eat an apple.

All sorts of cattle this dragon did eat
Some say he ate up trees,
And that the forests sure he would
Devour by degrees.
For houses and churches were to him
geese and turkeys
He ate all, and left none behind
But some stones, good sirs,
that he couldn't crack
Which on the hills you'll find.

Anonymous

223

THE CASTLE IN THE FIRE

The andirons were the dragons,
Set out to guard the gate
Of the old enchanted castle,
In the fire upon the grate.

We saw a turret window
Open a little space,
And frame, for just a moment,
A lady's lovely face;

Then, while we watched in wonder
From out the smoky veil,
A gallant knight came riding,
Dressed in coat of mail;

With slender lance a-tilting,
Thrusting with a skillful might,
He charged the crouching dragons –
Ah, 'twas a brilliant fight!

Then, in the roar and tumult,
The back log crashed in two,
And castle, knight and dragons
Were hidden from our view;

But, when the smoke had lifted,
We saw, to our delight,
Riding away together,
The lady and the knight.

Mary Jane Carr

PAPER BOATS

Day by day I float my paper boats one by one down the running stream.

In big black letters I write my name on them and the name of the village where I live.

I hope that someone in some strange land will find them and know who I am.

I load my little boats with shiuli flowers from our garden, and hope

that these blooms of dawn will be carried safely to land in the night.

I launch my paper boats and look up into the sky

and see the little clouds setting their white bulging sails.

I know not what playmate of mine in the sky sends them down the

air to race with my boats!

When night comes I bury my face in my arms and dream that my

paper boats float on and on under the midnight stars.

The fairies of sleep are sailing in them, and the lading is their baskets

full of dreams.

Rabindranath Tagore

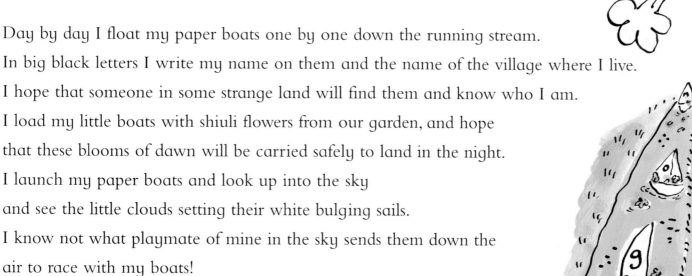

225

A SMALL DRAGON

I've found a small dragon in the woodshed.
Think it must have come from deep inside a forest
because it's damp and green and leaves
are still reflecting in its eyes.

I fed it on many things, tried grass,
the roots of stars, hazel-nut and dandelion,
but it stared up at me as if to say, I need
foods you can't provide.

It made a nest among the coal,
not unlike a bird's but larger,
it is out of place here
and is quite silent.

If you believed in it I would come
hurrying to your house to let you share my wonder,
but I want instead to see
if you yourself will pass this way.

Brian Patten

CATCH ME THE MOON, DADDY

Catch me the moon, Daddy,
Let it shine near me for a while,
Catch me the moon, Daddy,
I want to touch its smile.

The moon must shine from high above;
That's where it needs to stay
Among the stars, to guide them home
When they return from play.

So the bunny can find his supper,
So the mouse can scamper free,
So the hedgehog can make his forays,
So the birds can sleep in the tree.

And as for you, my child,
With slender silver thread
The moon will weave sweet dreams, so you
May slumber in your bed.

Griger Vitez

I LIKE TO STAY UP

I like to stay up
and listen
when big people talking
jumbie stories

I does feel
so tingly and excited
inside me

But when my mother say
"Girl, time for bed"

Then is when
I does feel a dread

Then is when
I does jump into me bed

Then is when
I does cover up
from me feet to me head

Then is when
I does wish I didn't listen
to no stupid jumbie story

Then is when
I does wish I did read
me book instead

Grace Nichols

228

MAGIC STORY OF FALLING ASLEEP

When the last giant came out of his cave
and his bones turned into the mountain
and his clothes turned into the flowers,

nothing was left but his tooth
which my dad took home in his truck
which my grandad carved into a bed

which my mum tucks me into at night
when I dream of the last giant
when I fall asleep on the mountain.

Nancy Willard

DREAMING SONGS

The powers I had won, beneath my bed I placed.
I lay upon them and lay down to sleep.
Then, in a little time, mysteriously there came to me beautiful songs,
Beautiful songs for the circling dance.

Papago Traditional Song

229

THE EVENING IS COMING

The evening is coming, the sun sinks to rest,
The birds are all flying straight home to their nests,
"Caw, caw," says the crow as he flies overhead,
It's time little children were going to bed.

Here comes the pony, his work is all done,
Down through the meadow he takes a good run,
Up go his heels – and down goes his head.
It's time little children were going to bed.

Anonymous

WINDY NIGHTS

Whenever the moon and stars are set,
Whenever the wind is high,
All night long in the dark and wet,
A man goes riding by.
Late in the night when the fires are out,
Why does he gallop and gallop about?

Whenever the trees are crying aloud,
And ships are tossed at sea,
By, on the highway, low and loud,
By at the gallop goes he.
By at the gallop he goes, and then
By he comes back at the gallop again.

Robert Louis Stevenson

Hush, little baby, don't say a word,
Papa's gonna buy you a mocking bird.
And if that mocking bird don't sing,
Papa's gonna buy you a diamond ring.

If that diamond ring turns brass,
Papa's gonna buy you a looking glass.
And if that looking glass gets broke,
Papa's gonna buy you a billy goat.

If that billy goat won't pull,
Papa's gonna buy you a cart and bull.
And if that cart and bull turn over,
Papa's gonna buy you a dog named Rover.

And if that dog named Rover won't bark,
Papa's gonna buy you a horse and cart.
And if that horse and cart fall down,
You'll still be the sweetest little baby in town.

Traditional

BLACK BATS

The sun is slowly departing.
It is slower in its setting.
Black bats will be swooping
when the sun is gone.
   That is all.

Papago Traditional Song

Cocks crow in the morn
To tell us to rise,
And he who lies late
Will never be wise;
For early to bed
And early to rise
Makes a man healthy
And wealthy and wise.

Anonymous

THE NIGHT WIND

Have you ever heard the wind go "Yoooooo"?
'Tis a pitiful sound to hear!
It seems to chill you through and through
With a strange and speechless fear.
'Tis the voice of the night that broods outside
When folk should be asleep,
And many and many's the time I've cried
To the darkness brooding far and wide
Over the land and the deep:
"Whom do you want, O lonely night,
That you wail the long hours through?"
And the night would say in its ghostly way:
"Yoooooooo! Yoooooooo! Yoooooooo!"

My mother told me long ago
(When I was a little tad)
That when the night went wailing so,
Somebody had been bad;
And then, when I was snug in bed,
Whither I had been sent,
With the blankets pulled up round my head,
I'd think of what my mother'd said,
And wonder what boy she meant!
And "Who's been bad today?" I'd ask
Of the wind that hoarsely blew,
And the voice would say in its meaningful way:
"Yoooooooo! Yoooooooo! Yoooooooo!"

That this was true I must allow –
You'll not believe it, though!
Yes, though I'm quite a model now,
I was not always so.
And if you doubt what things I say,
Suppose you make the test;
Suppose, when you've been bad some day
And up to bed are sent away
From mother and the rest –
Suppose you ask, "Who has been bad?"
And then you'll hear what's true;
For the wind
will moan in its ruefulest tone:
"Yoooooooo! Yoooooooo! Yoooooooo!"

Eugene Field

233

ALONE IN THE DARK

She has taken out the candle,
She has left me in the dark;
From the window not a glimmer,
From the fireplace not a spark.

I am frightened as I'm lying
All alone here in my bed,
And I've wrapped the clothes as closely
As I can around my head.

But what is it makes me tremble?
And why should I fear the gloom?
I am certain there is nothing
In the corners of the room.

Anonymous

Starlight, star bright,
First star I see tonight,
I wish I may, I wish I might,
Have the wish I wish tonight.

Anonymous

TWINKLE TWINKLE LITTLE STAR

Twinkle, twinkle, little star,
How I wonder what you are!
Up above the world so high,
Like a diamond in the sky.

In the dark blue sky you keep,
And often through my curtains peep,
For you never shut your eye,
'Til the sun is in the sky.

Jane Taylor

234

THE STAR IN THE PAIL

I took the pail for water when the sun was high
And left it in the shadow of the barn nearby.

When evening slippered over like the moth's brown wing,
I went to fetch the water from the cool wellspring.

The night was clear and warm and wide, and I alone
Was walking by the light of stars as thickly sown

As wheat across the prairie, or the first fall flakes,
Or spray upon the lawn – the kind the sprinkler makes.

But every star was far away as far can be,
With all the starry silence sliding over me.

And every time I stopped I set the pail down slow,
For when I stopped to pick the handle up to go

Of all the stars in heaven there was one to spare,
And he slivered in the water and I left him there.

David McCord

TWO IN BED

When my brother Tommy
Sleeps in bed with me,
He doubles up
And makes
himself
exactly
like
a
V

And 'cause the bed is not so wide,
A part of him is on my side.

A B Ross

BATHTIME

In goes the water,
Not too hot.
Squeeze out the bubble stuff,
In goes the lot.

In goes my whale
In goes my boat.
In go all the toys
That I can float.

Now my bath is ready
What else can there be?
I think I remember . . .
In goes ME.

Georgie Adams

SLEEPLESS NIGHTS

One night
when I was very little,
I couldn't sleep.

My mother came
and carried me downstairs
and stood with me
looking out of our window.

The street light was on outside,
and snow was whirling, swirling,
a dazzling white
around and around the street light.
And the ground
and trees
and bushes
were icy crystal white.

I remember that night,
with the snow
white, white, white,
and my mother's arms around me
warm and tight.

Charlotte Zolotow

SLEEP CHARMS

The rain is dripping fast; we sleep well, don't we?

At the river when we pitch camp, we hear the
    cicadas calling and doze off, don't we?

When it is windy and the tent flaps flap together,
    we sleep well, don't we?

When it is windy and the pine needles rustle,
    we sleep well, don't we?

Crow Traditional Song

237

KENTUCKY BABE

Skeeters are a-humming on the honeysuckle vine,

Sleep, Kentucky Babe!

Sandman is a-coming to this little babe of mine,

Sleep, Kentucky Babe!

Silvery moon is shining in the heavens up above,

Bobolink is pining for his little lady love,

You are mighty lucky,

Babe of old Kentucky,

Close your eyes in sleep.

Fly away,

Fly away, Kentucky Babe, fly away to rest,

Fly away,

Lay your tiny curly head on your mommy's breast

Hm . . . Hm . . .

Close your eyes in sleep.

Anonymous

COMFORTING SONG

Do not cry, little one.

Your father will fetch you.

Father is coming as soon as he

has made his new harpoon head.

Do not cry, little one.

Do not weep.

Inuit Traditional Song

GRANDPA BEAR'S LULLABY

The night is long
But fur is deep.
You will be warm
In winter sleep.

The food is gone
But dreams are sweet
And they will be
Your winter meat.

The cave is dark
But dreams are bright
And they will serve
As winter light.

Sleep, my little cubs, sleep.

Jane Yolen

ALL THROUGH THE NIGHT

Sleep, my babe, lie still and slumber,
All through the night,
Guardian angels God will lend thee,
All through the night;
Soft, the drowsy hours are creeping,
Hill and vale in slumber steeping,
Mother, dear, her watch is keeping,
All through the night.

Traditional

NORSE LULLABY

The sky is dark and the hills are white
As the storm-king speeds from the north tonight;
And this is the song the storm-king sings,
As over the world his cloak he flings:
"Sleep, sleep, little one, sleep,"
He rustles his wings and gruffly sings:
"Sleep, little one, sleep."
On yonder mountainside a vine
Clings at the foot of a mother pine;
The tree bends over the trembling thing,
And only the vine can hear her sing:
"Sleep, sleep, little one, sleep –
What shall you fear when I am here?
Sleep, little one, sleep."
The king may sing in his bitter flight,
The tree may croon to the vine tonight,
But the little snowflake at my breast
Liketh the song I sing the best –
Sleep, sleep, little one, sleep;
Weary thou art, a-next my heart
Sleep, little one, sleep.

Eugene Field

QUESTIONS AT NIGHT

Why
Is the sky?
What starts the thunder overhead?
Who makes the crashing noise?
Are the angels falling out of bed?
Are they breaking all their toys?

Why does the sun go down so soon?
Why do the night-clouds crawl
Hungrily up to the new-laid moon
And swallow it, shell and all?

If there's a Bear among the stars
As all the people say,
Won't he jump over those Pasture-bars
And drink up the Milky Way?

Does every star that happens to fall
Turn into a fire-fly?
Can't it ever get back to Heaven at all?
And why
Is the sky?

Louis Untermeyer

The moon peeped through the window.
I was lying in my bed.
It was very bright that starry night,
So I opened a book and read.

Finola Akister

ARE ALL THE GIANTS DEAD?

Are all the giants dead?
And all the witches fled?
Am I quite safe in bed?

Giants and witches all are fled.
My child, thou art quite safe in bed.

Hilary Pepler

RAINDROP

Raindrops a-falling from the skies,
Tired and sleepy, close your eyes.
Tired and sleepy
While the skies are weeping,
Weeping and singing you their lullabies.
Tired and sleepy,
While the skies are weeping,
Weeping and singing you their lullabies.

Slovak Lullaby

HOW MANY MILES TO BABYLON?

How many miles to Babylon?
Threescore and ten, sir.

Can I get there by candlelight?
Oh yes, and back again, sir.

If your heels are nimble and light,
You may get there by candlelight.

Traditional

THE MOON

The moon has a face like the clock in the hall;
She shines on thieves on the garden wall,
On streets and fields and harbour quays,
And birdies asleep in the forks of the trees.

The squalling cat and the squeaking mouse,
The howling dog by the door of the house,
The bat that lies in bed at noon,
All love to be out by the light of the moon.

But all of the things that belong to the day
Cuddle to sleep to be out of her way;
And flowers and children close their eyes
Till up in the morning the sun shall rise.

Robert Louis Stevenson

GOOD NIGHT

We turn out the lights
and the colour is gone.
The shapes are gone.
The desk,
the chair
with tomorrow's clothes laid out,
the books
in the bookcase,
the crayons
on the floor,
the bright curtains,
the red rug
are covered by friendly dark.

Only with closed eyes
can you see now.

Charlotte Zolotow

UPHILL

Does the road wind uphill all the way?
Yes, to the very end.
Will the day's journey take the whole long day?
From morn to night, my friend.

But is there for the night a resting-place?
A roof for when the slow, dark hours begin.
May not the darkness hide it from my face?
You cannot miss that inn.

Shall I meet other wayfarers at night?
Those who have gone before.
Then must I knock, or call when just in sight?
They will not keep you waiting at that door.

Shall I find comfort, travel-sore and weak?
Of labour you shall find the sum.
Will there be beds for me and all who seek?
Yea, beds for all who come.

Christina Rossetti

LADY MOON

Lady Moon, Lady Moon, where are you roving?
Over the sea.
Lady Moon, Lady Moon, whom are you loving?
All that love me.

Are you not tired with rolling, and never
Resting to sleep?
Why look so pale, and so sad, as for ever
Wishing to weep?

Ask me not this, little child, if you love me;
You are too bold;
I must obey my dear father above me,
And do as I'm told.

Lady Moon, Lady Moon, where are you roving?
Over the sea.
Lady Moon, Lady Moon, whom are you loving?
All that love me.

Richard Monckton Miles, Lord Houghton

245

SONG TO STRAIGHTEN A BAD DREAM

All is beautiful where I dream.

All is beautiful where I dream.

I dream amid the dawn and all is beautiful.

I dream amid the white corn and all is beautiful.

I dream amid the beautiful goods and all is beautiful.

I dream amid the mixed waters and all is beautiful.

I dream amid all the pollens and all is beautiful.

I dream that all is beautiful.

Navajo Traditional Song

LULLABY

Someone would like to have you for her child

but you are mine.

Someone would like to rear you on a costly mat

but you are mine.

Someone would like to place you on a camel blanket

but you are mine.

I have you to rear on a torn old mat.

Someone would like to have you as her child

but you are mine.

Traditional African Lullaby

LULLABY

The long canoe
Toward the shadowy shore,
One . . . two . . .
Three . . . four . . .
The paddle dips,
Turns in the wake,
Pauses, then
Forward again,
Water drips
From the blade to the lake.
Nothing but that,
No sound of wings;
The owl and bat
Are velvet things.
No wind awakes,
No fishes leap,
No rabbits creep
Among the brakes.

The long canoe
At the shadowy shore,
One . . . two . . .
Three . . . four . . .
A murmur now
Under the prow
Where rushes bow
To let us through.
One . . . two . . .
Upon the shore,
Three . . . four . . .
Upon the lake,
No one's awake,
No one's awake,
One . . .
Two . . .
No one,
Not even
You.

Robert Hillyer

THE DARK

I don't like the dark coming down on my head
It feels like a blanket thrown over the bed
I don't like the dark coming down on my head

I don't like the dark coming down over me
It feels like the room's full of things I can't see
I don't like the dark coming down over me

There isn't enough light from under the door
It only just reaches the edge of the floor
There isn't enough light from under the door

I wish that my dad hadn't put out the light
It feels like there's something that's just out of sight
I wish that my dad hadn't put out the light

But under the bedclothes it's warm and secure
You can't see the ceiling you can't see the floor
Yes, under the bedclothes it's warm and secure
So I think I'll stay here till it's daylight once more.

Adrian Henri

Sleep, baby, sleep,
Your father keeps the sheep;
Your mother shakes a little tree,
A dream falls gently down for thee:
     Sleep, baby, sleep.

Sleep, baby, sleep,
Your father keeps the sheep;
Your mother guards the lambs this night,
And keeps them safe till morning light:
     Sleep, baby, sleep.

Sleep, baby, sleep,
In heaven lie the sheep;
The little lambs like stars of gold,
The moon's the shepherd of the fold:
     Sleep, baby, sleep.

Anonymous

LULLABY

Sleep, my baby, sleep!
Once there was a sheep.

When its fleece was shorn,
the sheep could not keep warm.

A kind man going to the fair
gave the sheep his coat to wear.

Now the sheep is warm and snug,
Wrapped in a coat thick as a rug.

Sleep, my baby, sleep.
Once there was a sheep.

Christian Morgenstern

A CHILD'S THOUGHT

At seven, when I go to bed,
I find such pictures in my head:
Castles with dragons prowling round,
Gardens where magic fruits are found;
Fair ladies prisoned in a tower,
Or lost in an enchanting bower;
While gallant horsemen ride by streams
That border all this land of dreams
I find, so clearly in my head
At seven, when I go to bed.

Robert Louis Stevenson

SLEEP SONG

Listen now,
listen now to the birds,
how they sing,
singing all around this tree.
Listen to the water,
how nicely the water is roaring
through the rocks and down the hollow.
Listen to the wind,
how sweetly it sounds
rushing through the trees.

Potawatomi Traditional Song

Dance to your daddie,
My bonnie laddie,
Dance to your daddie,
My bonnie lamb.

You shall get a fishie
In a little dishie,
And you'll get an eggie
And a bit of ham.

You shall get a coatie,
And a pair of breekies,
You shall get a fishie
When the boats come hame.

You shall get a pony
Fit to ride for ony,
And you'll get a whippie
For to make him gang.

Dance to your daddie,
My bonnie laddie,
Dance to your daddie,
My bonnie lamb.

Traditional

NIGHT PRAYER

This night
We have fulfilled the thoughts of our fathers.
Always with one thought
We shall live.
My children,
This night
Your children,
Your families,
Happily you will pass on their roads.
Happily we shall always live.

Zuni Traditional Song

That's all! Time to go now!
But before I say goodbye …

here are some riddles for you to solve. If you really can't guess,
turn the book upside down to see the answers.

Light as a feather,
Nothing in it,
But few can hold it
For even a minute.

A person's breath.

What is the difference
Between a dancer and a duck?
To solve this riddle
You will need a lot of luck.

A dancer goes quick on her legs,
A duck goes quack on her eggs.

Round and round the rugged rock
The ragged rascal ran.
How many R's are there in that?
Now tell me if you can.

"There aren't any R's in "that.""

Many eyes,
Never cries.

A potato.

What is it you always see
In earth, in fire, in smoke, in tea?
It is in your feet,
It is in your head,
You will even find it in your bed.

The letter "e".

As I was going to St Ives,
I met a man with seven wives,
Each wife had seven sacks,
Each sack had seven cats,
Each cat had seven kits –
Kits, cats, sacks, and wives,
How many were going to St Ives?

One person was going to St Ives;
the others were coming from St Ives.

Feed it,
It will grow high.
Give it water,
It will die.

Fire.

Goodbye!

252

INDEX

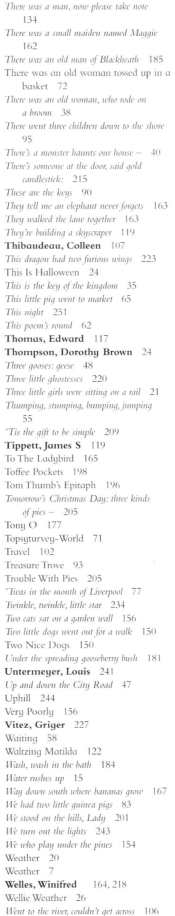

ACKNOWLEDGEMENTS

The Publisher would like to thank the following for permission to use copyright material: Orion Children's Books for seven poems by Georgie Adams from *A Year Full of Stories*; Penguin Books for six poems by Finola Akister from *Before You Grow Up* (Viking Kestrel); Thomas Nelson for "Racing the Wind" by Moira Andrew from *Racing the Wind*; Faber and Faber for "How many apples grow on the tree" by George Barker from *Runes and Rhymes and Tunes and Chimes*; Caxton Printers for "Beside the Line" by Edna Becker from *Pickpocket Songs*; Marian Reiner for "Growing Up" by Harry Behn from *The Little Hill*, copyright 1949, renewed 1977 by Alice L. Behn; Peters Fraser & Dunlop on behalf of the Estate of Hilaire Belloc for "The Frog" from *Complete Verse*; Jacqueline Brown for "Wellie Weather"; David Higham Associates for "Figgie Hobbin" by Charles Causley from *Collected Poems*; Sarah Matthews for two poems by Stanley Cook; Faber and Faber for "Waiting" by Sue Cowling from *What is a Kumquat?*; Sheila Colman for "The Shark" by Lord Alfred Douglas; Samuel French on behalf of the John Drinkwater Estate for "The Postman"; the Literary Trustees of Walter de la Mare and the Society of Authors for "Snow" and "Tartary" from *The Complete Poems of Walter de la Mare*; HarperCollins Publishers for "My Cat" by Barbara Esbensen from *Who Shrank My Grandmother's House?*; Margo Ewart for two poems by Gavin Ewart from *Like It Or Not* (Bodley Head); New Directions Publishing Corp. for "Fortune" by Lawrence Ferlinghetti from *A Coney Island of the Mind*; John Johnson for "Night Walk" by Max Fatchen from *Songs for My Dog and Other People* (Kestrel Books); John Foster for "My Front Tooth" from *Making Waves* (OUP) and "Ten Dancing Dinosaurs", "The Central Heating" and "The Secrets Box" from *Four O'Clock Friday* (OUP); Macmillan Publishers for "Guinea Pigs" by Rumer Godden from *From Cockrow to Starlight*; Carcanet Press for "I'd Love to be a Fairy's Child" by Robert Graves from *Complete Poems*; Rogers, Coleridge & White for "A Poem for my Cat" by Adrian Henri from *The Phantom Lollipop Lady* (Methuen) and "The Dark" by Adrian Henri from *Rhinestone Rhino* (Methuen); Alfred A. Knopf for "Lullaby" by Robert Hillyer from *Poems for Music*, copyright 1947, renewed 1975 by Francesca P. Hillyer and Elizabeth V. Hillyer, and "April Rain Song" by Langston Hughes from *Collected Poems*, copyright 1974 by the Estate of Langston Hughes; Mike Jubb for "Aunty Aggie" and "Where Can It Be?"; Evans Bros for "What do you collect?" by Wes Magee from *All the Day Through*; Margaret Mahy for "Cat in the Dark"; David Higham Associates for "Haunted" by William Mayne from *Ghosts* (Hamish Hamilton); Little, Brown and Co. for six poems by David McCord from *One at a Time*; Scribner, a division of Simon & Schuster, for "The Crows" by David McCord, copyright 1934, renewed 1962 by David McCord; Carcanet Press for "Beside the Line" by Ian McMillan; Walker Books for "Said the Boy to the Dinosaur" by Colin McNaughton from *Who's Been Sleeping in my Porridge?*, and "The Garden's Full of Witches" by Colin McNaughton from *There's An Awful Lot of Weirdos in our Neighbourhood*; Marian Reiner for "Weather" by Eve Merriam from *Catch a Little Rhyme*, copyright 1966, renewed 1994 by Dee Michel, and for "Windshield Wiper" by Eve Merriam from *Chortles* (Morrow Jr Books); Peters Fraser & Dunlop for "What to do when you meet a Giant" by Adrian Mitchell from *Coffee* (Bloodaxe Books); Cynthia Mitchell for "Hank" from *Madtail, Miniwhale* (Viking Kestrel); David Higham Associates for "Magic Carpet" and "Lollipop Poem" by Tony Mitton; Hodder and Stoughton for "What Really Happened" by John Mole from *Hot Air*; Michael Neugebauer & Nord-Sud Verlag for "Lullaby" and "The Cold" by Christian Morgenstern from *Lullabies and Lyrics*; Rogers, Coleridge & White for "A Lesson" by Brian Morse from *Plenty of Time* (Bodley Head); Curtis Brown for "Sugarcake Bubble" by Grace Nichols from *No Hickory No Dickory No Dock* (Viking), and "I Like to Stay Up" by Grace Nichols from *Come On Into My Tropical Garden* (A & C Black); Rogers, Coleridge & White for "Moon", "Postbox" and "Scatterbrain" by Gareth Owen from *My Granny is a Sumo Wrestler* (Young Lions), and "Winter Days" by Gareth Owen from *Wordscapes* (OUP); Egmont Children's Books for "Treasure Trove" and "Painting" by Irene Rawnsley from *Ask a Silly Question* (Methuen Children's Books), and "Liquorice Bootlaces" by Irene Rawnsley from *The House of a Hundred Cats* (Methuen Children's Books); Laura Cecil for "The Black Pebble" by James Reeves from *Complete Poems for Children* (Heinemann); Orion and J.M.Dent for "Little Train" by Paul Rogers; David Higham Associates for "The Dustman" by Clive Sansom from *The Golden Unicorn*, and for "The King of China's Daughter" by Edith Sitwell from *The Wooden Pegasus* (Blackwell); Random House for "Bath", "Christmas in the Sun" and "Dance" by Pauline Stewart from *Singing Down the Breadfruit* (Bodley Head); Macmillan Publishers for "Paper Boats" by Rabindrath Tagore; Colleen Thibaudeau for "Balloon" from *Madtail, Miniwhale* (Viking Kestrel); Harcourt Brace for "Questions at Night" by Louis Untermeyer from *Rainbow in the Sky*, copyright 1935, renewed 1963 by Louis Untermeyer; Colin West for "Me and Amanda" from *What to do with a Wobble-de-Woo* (Century Hutchinson); Random House for "Fishing for Rainbows" and "Toffee Pockets" by Jeanne Willis from *Toffee Pockets* (Bodley Head), and for "Cross Canary" by Gina Wilson from *Jim-Jam Pyjamas* (Jonathan Cape); Curtis Brown NY for "When I Grow Up" by William Wise; Harcourt Brace for "Good Night", "Leopard in the Zoo", "Sleepless Nights" and "The Pond" by Charlotte Zolotow from *Everything Glistens and Everything Sings*; Scott Treimel for "People" by Charlotte Zolotow from *All That Sunlight* (Harper & Row). The Publisher would like to hear from any copyright holders who could not be traced, and will be happy to include a full acknowledgement in any future edition.